THE DRAGON RIDER

WHO SAVED THE WORLD

THE GOLDEN EGG

TED DEKKER & RACHELLE DEKKER

Copyright © 2024 by Ted Dekker

All rights reserved. No part of this book may be reproduced in any manner whatsoever without written permission, except in the case of brief quotations embodied in critical articles and reviews.

ISBN (Paperback Edition): 979-8-9888509-9-1

Also Available in *The Dragon Rider who Saved the World* trilogy:

The Unknown Path (Book Two)
ISBN: 979-8-9909639-0-0 (Paperback Edition)

Rise of the Fire Walker (Book Three)
ISBN: 979-8-9909639-1-7 (Paperback Edition)

Published by:
Scripturo
350 E. Royal Lane, Suite 150
Irving, TX 75039

Cover art and design by Manuel Preitano

Printed in China by Artful Dragon Press, a U.S. Corporation

CHAPTER 1

EMILIA HANDED A STRAIGHT PIN to her mother, who took it without looking, the motion second nature after a lifetime of making alterations. Kneeling, Emilia let her eyes trail up the shimmery silver fabric of the gown and landed on the girl wearing it. Ruth held perfectly still, her long blonde curls tucked behind her ears. Her delicate face, housing bright blue eyes, looked forward. A splash of light freckles littered the bridge of her nose and the tops of her cheeks. Mother worked on the waistline at Ruth's back, pinning it to fit Ruth's petite frame.

The bodice was fitted with small, capped sleeves and a sweetheart neckline. The skirt billowed and fell to the tops of Ruth's matching silver shoes. The fabric was soft and airy. Emilia thought about the way it would flutter when Ruth walked. The way it would dance as she spun. It paired beautifully with the gold, metal band that cuffed Ruth's forearm.

Very few people wore bands made of metal, reserved for the most elite in Capital City. Emilia's white fabric band symbolized her humble place in society. Every member of Capital City was required to identify their status with a colored band whenever they were in public. The law ensured safety and peace. It maintained order, as all the laws did.

Emilia's fingers pressed her plain, gray dress, sewn by her mother's hand at home. The comfortable cotton was incapable of airy, fluttering movement, but she knew to be grateful because many others throughout Capital City had less. Still, she couldn't stop the small beat of envy that pulsed near her heart. She would never wear a beautiful dress as Ruth wore now. Her path was clear. She would assist her mother, the royal family seamstress, until she was old enough to take her place.

If she closed her eyes, she could see the steps before her. They held little surprise and less mystery. Even at thirteen, she knew to be grateful for this too. Many struggled to find a fruitful future; hers would come without strife. To want more was selfish. To covet Ruth's life—detestable.

She rebuked her thoughts, shame curling up her

Chapter 1

spine. Ruth was Emilia's best friend and the daughter of Martin Cornell, the Grand Master and ruler of Capital City. One day, Ruth would take her father's place. As his only child, she would lead, keeping Capital City safe and orderly, continuing to follow the laws the Order established 150 years ago. That was Ruth's path, as clearly marked as Emilia's.

Chaos ruled the world before Sylas, a great warlord, defeated the darkness of the skies, established the Order, and became the first Grand Master. According to the Histories, before the Order, groups that tried to rule humanity only destroyed it. The scaled creatures that devoured the hearts and minds of men were even more dangerous. Sylas had saved humanity from the dragons—demons Emilia was too afraid to even think about.

"Finished," Mother said, yanking Emilia from her thoughts.

"Oh good," Ruth exhaled. "I was holding my breath for so long I started to feel faint."

"I wish you would've fainted," Emilia teased. "That would've made for such a good story."

"Next time then," Mother said with a wink to Emilia. She tapped Ruth's shoulder affectionately. "Out of this now, so I can take it with me."

Ruth grabbed fistfuls of the gown on either side of

the long skirt and headed for the bathroom. Emilia and her mother collected the tools of their trade—pins, measuring tapes, chalk, and scissors—and returned them to their basket. Mother grabbed the handle and tucked it over the crook of her elbow.

"I need to stop by the Grand Master's suite to ensure his new trousers fit," she said.

"Do you need help?" Emilia asked, hoping her voice communicated that she didn't want to help.

Her mother gave a soft huff and cocked her head slightly. "As my apprentice, you'll need to be able to sew dresses *and* pants."

"I practice on Father," Emilia started, "And I can stay behind and collect Ruth's dress, so you don't have to wait." It was a poor excuse, but by now Mother knew Emilia just wanted to spend time with her friend before they headed home for the day.

Mother exhaled with a slight shake of her head. "Fine, but I expect you to be at the northern gate in thirty minutes, not a moment later."

Emilia nodded and smiled as her mother turned and left the bedroom. Ruth emerged from her bathroom a second later, the silver gown carefully hanging over her arm. She handed the dress to Emilia.

"Where's Silvia?" she asked.

"Gone to fix your father's pants," Emilia replied.

Chapter 1

"And you gave up that esteemed honor to be with me?" Ruth teased as Emilia carefully folded and wrapped the gown in burlap, to protect it as she transported it back home for her mother to alter.

"Never forget the sacrifice I've made for you today," Emilia said playfully.

With a giggle, Ruth threw herself back onto her large four-poster bed, the mattress pillow-topped and covered in a snow-white blanket. Sage-colored pillows decorated the headboard, and a soft wool blanket draped the foot. The bed was large enough to swallow both girls in lushness. The entire room was that way, large enough for Emilia's simple, single-level home to fit inside.

Emilia had spent hours in this room, yet she was still taken with its beauty. Delicate silver sconces on white walls gave off just the right amount of light. A small, crystal chandelier cast dancing sparkles across the wooden floors. A large, sky-blue rug took up the floor's center and warmed bare feet. An oak armoire sat against the east wall, a matching trunk at the foot of the bed, and a small writing desk with a yellow, velvet chair beside the wooden entry door.

Fresh flowers always stood inside a crystal vase on the desk, making the room smell like rain and pollen. This was one of Emilia's favorite places. Emilia didn't have many friends. She didn't like talking to people she didn't know and was happy with her parents and Ruth being her closest—really only—companions.

Unlike Emilia, Ruth had many friends. She often rushed around with the other young girls that lived in First Ring, but also spent hours with Emilia. Emilia couldn't help but feel honored that Ruth cared for her so much. Especially since they lived such different lives.

"I will never forget," Ruth said. "I owe you a great debt."

Emilia smiled, sitting beside Ruth on the bed. She watched her friend's expression darken and knew she was thinking about next week. "Most people enjoy their birthdays. Turning fourteen."

"No, I refuse," Ruth said, flipping over to her stomach and propping herself on her elbows. "I won't age anymore. I just won't do it."

"People grow up, Ruth."

"*People* don't have to rule a city when they do."

Silence fell between the girls. When she decided to speak, Emilia kept her voice light. "Well, that's not for a while. And think of all the good you'll do."

"That's the whole point, Emilia. I don't want to think about it. Father says I should start taking my future more seriously. 'Fourteen is one year closer to eighteen,' he keeps reminding me." Ruth mocked her father's tone,

Chapter 1

grabbed a pillow, and laid it over her face in dramatic fashion. "Everything will change," she grumbled through the pillow.

Order law stated that by the end of an heir's eighteenth year, they must be betrothed and participate in most governing sessions. This ensured if anything happened to the Grand Master, the heir would be ready to assume the role. It also meant less freedom; and days filled with political, tactical, and financial meetings. No time for running, playing, reading, and daydreaming, all of which made up the essence of Ruth.

Where Emilia was cautious and timid, Ruth was spontaneous and free. They were opposites in many ways. Emilia was tanned with dark hair and chocolate eyes. Tall and lean. Ruth was petite and blonde, with a fair complexion and crystal blue eyes.

Emilia held her tongue, whereas Ruth said whatever she was thinking—as long as it wasn't against the law, of course. Emilia was thoughtful with her words, while Ruth was passionate with hers. Ruth's constant laugh was contagious, while Emilia struggled to see the joy. Ruth was always telling Emilia she was too serious for her age, and Emilia was always trying to ensure Ruth's passion didn't get her in trouble.

Both girls followed the law; to do anything different would be an unforgivable offense to the Order they respected and feared. But Ruth had a way of living that seemed free, even inside the stringent laws.

Emilia couldn't understand the burden of Ruth's future, but she did expect to experience more heaviness as she aged. Her father had unknowingly reinforced this concern. Worry and her father hadn't always paired, but in the last six months, he'd ... changed.

Memories of hushed conversations between her parents echoed in her head; conversations that could get her father into deep trouble. To question the Order and its laws was dangerous. But to speak of the Guardians was deadly. The group of rebels disregarded the protection of the Order and tried to twist people's minds with heresy. It was said that they believed in dragons.

A shiver coursed Emilia's spine and she tried to banish the rebellious ideas. She must have misheard her father. He would never endanger himself and his family with such heresy.

"What are you thinking about?" Ruth asked.

Emilia turned her eyes toward her closest friend and swallowed.

Ruth had removed her pillow and was looking at Emilia with concern. "I can tell something is wrong."

"It's nothing," Emilia lied as she tried to smile.

"You're lying," Ruth said. She sat up and reached

Chapter 1

for Emilia's hand. "I can feel the worry coming off you. You can tell me."

Emilia shouldn't tell anyone about her father. The words he'd spoken were forbidden. Punishable by banishment.

Or death.

But as Ruth held Emilia's eyes, they filled with tears. She couldn't believe she was getting so emotional. That, too, was dangerous. Ruth was the daughter of the Grand Master! Telling her anything would endanger her father.

But Ruth was her best friend. Her only friend! And the weight of carrying her father's words was tiresome.

"You can trust me, Emilia. I only want your happiness," Ruth said with a small squeeze of Emilia's hand.

"It's my father," Emilia started, her voice a low whisper.

"Is he alright? Is he sick or something?"

"No, but he's different."

"Different how? Is he mistreating you or your mother?" Ruth's accusation felt angry.

"No!" Emilia said. "Of course, not that. He would never!"

"Well then, what?"

Emilia swallowed, and her fingers started to quake.

"Emilia, you're shaking. Tell me what's wrong."

"He's speaking about things he shouldn't."

Ruth went still and her eyes grew wide.

"He mentioned a man in the desert and the Guardians. I've heard him ask questions that go outside the law and . . ." Emilia wasn't sure she could continue. "And he talked about . . . he talked about . . ."

Dragons, Emilia thought but couldn't say.

Ruth held a finger to Emilia's lips. "Don't say it. Not here or anywhere."

Fear rammed Emilia's chest as she drew her eyes to Ruth's terrified gaze.

"No wonder you're afraid," Ruth said in a harsh whisper. "I wish you hadn't told me."

"You asked me to," Emilia said softly.

Ruth's face eased and she nodded. "I know, I'm sorry. That isn't what I thought you were going to say."

"I'm sorry," Emilia said. "I didn't mean to cause you trouble."

Ruth hugged Emilia tight and sighed. "I'm sorry, it was just shocking." When Ruth pulled away, she gave Emilia a tight smile.

Ruth pushed herself off the bed.

"Let's get some fresh air." She grabbed Emilia's arm, sweetly tugging her to follow. Emilia obeyed, and the girls pushed through the large, double, glass doors that led to Ruth's balcony. Her room sat high in the Central

Chapter 1

Tower that overlooked the city.

Ruth looped her arm through Emilia's as the girls pressed against the stone railing. The fear in Emilia's chest softened. Capital City was located in a fertile valley and housed nearly sixty thousand people. Harsh desert surrounded the city, and everyone knew about the vicious windstorms and grueling sun beyond the safe boundaries.

One main road exited Capital City to the east. The closest neighboring city, also under the rule of the order, was five days away by horseback. Only desert stretched in every other direction. Leaving Capital City was prohibited without permission from the Grand Master, so very few people ventured beyond its borders.

The day was warm, bathed in the early afternoon sun. Like the cross-section of a tree trunk, the city was divided into six rings. Each ring displayed its wealth and status level. With the Central Tower building at the wealthy center, the Sixth Ring was the poorest and most populated, with dirt-and-mud streets, and homes stacked so close and high it looked as if a strong wind might flatten them. Those who lived there wore armbands of brown sackcloth, the most accessible material.

The Fifth and Fourth Rings weren't much better, but wood and cinderblocks made the homes sturdier. Their armbands were also brown, but some who lived there could afford richer material. They too were packed to capacity, seemingly living on top of one another.

The Third Ring, where Emilia lived, was starkly different from the outer rings. Its homes were well-constructed, and most had gardens. Some roads were paved. Residents donned white armbands and held jobs working for the Central Tower, the Order members, the high stables, and so forth. But the ring was bland compared to the glamour of the Second and First Rings, which were characterized by decadence.

Painted stone walls surrounded massive homes and private stables. Most had lawns with colorful flowers and sprouting foliage. Pristine white schools and medical facilities filled the landscape. All armbands were silver and gold, mostly metal or silk.

Only from this high vantage point could someone see the disparities so clearly. Emilia's stomach turned. She knew the ways of the Order were just and right, but she couldn't shake the feeling of *wrongness* at the sight below. Guilt swept through her. Nothing the Order did was wrong.

"Emilia," Ruth said.

"Yes?" Emilia turned to face her friend.

"Promise me you won't tell anyone else about your father."

Chapter 1

The fear that had nearly evaporated rushed back into Emilia's chest.

"I just don't want anything to happen to you," Ruth said. Tears brimmed in her eyes.

"I won't say anything. I promise," Emilia said.

Ruth gave her a nod and laid her head on Emilia's shoulder.

CHAPTER 2

TWO DAYS LATER, Emilia followed her mother through the north gate as they left the Central Tower. They'd just delivered the altered dress to Ruth. Emilia was afraid that things would be different between her and Ruth since Emilia's confession, but they seemed normal. Ruth had been pretty quiet today, but she said she was getting a cold. Her quiet demeanor was just that then, Emilia thought.

The Central Tower was a four-story structure, made of stone walls painted white to symbolize peace, and had marble floors throughout. The northern entry was an arch twenty feet high and wide enough for a horse-drawn cart. The Order Guards, several hundred men and women who protected the tower and the Grand Master, watched the entrance constantly.

They wore stern expressions, armor, and black

armbands. They made Emilia shiver, their eyes watching as all passed in and out of the Central Tower. The Order's insignia; a thick, perfectly braided rope; framed the archway behind her. Its message was clear: Woven together, we are solid and unbreakable, but if one strand falls out of place, we could fray and break. The inscription *In Order we find peace and safety. Outside we find death* was etched in graceful lettering above the insignia.

Emilia followed Silvia as they descended the wide marble staircase toward the paved road and the Treasury. It was Sunday, collection day. The Order oversaw and operated eleven Treasury buildings. There were two in each ring except for the Sixth, which had only one despite the Sixth Ring containing the largest population. Emilia imagined the lines for that Treasury building must be very long. It was the most prone to riots, but they were easily crushed by the Order.

Throughout the week, individuals received notes in exchange for work, and on Sundays, at the Treasury, they traded these notes for tokens. They used these tokens to buy everyday goods: food, fabric, household supplies, and more. Tokens were also bartered for electricity and water. Emilia didn't want to think about what would happen to anyone who didn't have enough tokens to trade for water, but that didn't happen. Did it?

Chapter 2

Emilia stood quietly as her mother collected their family's tokens, then followed as they left the Treasury building in First Ring. The journey home was half an hour, a walk they had done thousands of times. She could probably get home with her eyes closed.

The elegant homes of First and Second Ring changed and shrank as they crossed into the outskirts of Second Ring and into Third. Here, the spacing between homes decreased, the yards became fewer and smaller, and the buildings weren't spotless. But Emilia took comfort here. It was home.

They rounded the corner onto their street. They were lucky to live on a paved road. Many didn't, even in Third Ring. Identical homes, single-story, white-brick structures connected in rows of ten, lined both sides of the road. It wasn't much, but it was comforting and homey. Warm in the winter and cool with the summer-night breeze. It was the only place Emilia had ever lived and she'd always felt safe.

Emilia beat her mother to the front door, marked by the number four, and used her key to unlock the unit. She pushed open the door, stepped inside, and flipped on the overhead light. The small kitchen had space for a four-seater table, which Emilia's father had built. Behind the kitchen, a bathroom with a pedestal sink and clawfoot bathtub separated two small, identical bedrooms. In the modest living area, a fireplace nestled in the back wall. To one side was a dark green, plush chair; and a single reading light. To the other was a maroon couch.

There, sitting on the couch, was her father, home early.

Emilia stopped as he looked up with tired eyes and a pale face. He stood, towering over six feet, and rushed toward them as Silvia stepped through the entrance and closed the front door. She too stopped, surprised by his presence.

"Korin?" she said. "What are you doing home this early?"

Her father reached around Emilia to flip the light off. Dark gray swallowed the room.

"Dad . . ." Emilia started, but he touched her lips to shush her.

"Shh. We don't have much time."

"Korin, what is this?" Silvia demanded.

Her father grabbed Silvia's arm, yanking her with him as he moved away from Emilia. She stayed where she was, stunned and confused as her parents entered their small kitchen, voices low and harsh. Korin held Silvia's shoulders as she looked up, shaking her head.

Emilia got her height from her father. And his complexion. And his eyes. Something broke in her

Chapter 2

chest, anxiety filling her. *This isn't right,* she thought. *Something's wrong.* The air thinned like it sensed something was coming.

"You must stop," Silvia snapped. Emilia heard the fear in her voice. Silvia tried to push Korin away, but he held her firm.

"You must listen to me!" her father begged. "If anything happens you—"

"No! I won't accept that," her mother cried.

"Mom," Emilia said softly, "Dad, what's happening?"

Her mother dropped her eyes to the floor as her father's gaze, filled with worry and sadness, found Emilia's. She took a step toward him. "Please, Dad."

"I love you, Em," he said. "With all my heart."

Emilia opened her mouth, unsure what to say, but never got a chance to speak. The door behind her burst open and four compliance officers stepped inside. Dressed in black, they pounded across the wood floor in heavy combat boots. The red armbands were stark against their black sleeves, with knives strapped along their belt and thighs. Black helmets with tinted visors blocked most of their faces, leaving only their mouths visible. They terrified Emilia.

"Korin Harker," one of the guards said, his voice low and intimidating.

Korin moved to stand between them and his wife,

and Emilia rushed to her mother. The compliance officers didn't wait for Korin to respond. They took tight hold of his biceps, one on either side of Korin's tall frame.

"You're under arrest," an officer said.

"For what crime?" Silvia said.

"For treason against the Order," another answered, stepping before her mother as her father was led away.

"Follow us," the officer commanded.

"We've done nothing," Silvia said, taking Emilia's hand.

"Now," the officer said, prodding Emilia in the back.

Fear like lead filled her shoes, but her mother tugged her along as they followed the compliance officers out of their home.

CHAPTER 3

EMILIA SAT IN A COLD METAL CHAIR, the only piece of furniture in the gray concrete room. She couldn't shake her fear. It was like a boulder sitting on her chest, making breathing hard. A monster crouched on her back, whispering terrible things.

Your father is doomed.

He broke the law.

You know what happens to those who break the law.

After dragging them from their home, the compliance officers placed her father into a locked cell on the back of a horse-drawn cart. She and her mother were shoved into a second, open cart with wooden benches. They hurried toward the First Tier, Emilia and her mother's cart splitting from her father's as they neared the tower. Emilia didn't know where they were taking him, but her heart broke.

They were led into the Central Tower, from where they'd come less than an hour earlier. This time, the eyes of the Order Guards watched them with disgust as the compliance officers guided them up the steps to a secure room on the bottom floor.

"You, in there," one of the guards snapped, shoving Emilia into a room.

She stumbled in, as they hustled her into the cell and pushed her into the corner.

The guard faced Emilia, leaning in. "Tell us what you know about your father's involvement with the Guardians."

"I don't know anything," she said.

"Tell us who else he's spoken to."

"I don't know."

"Lying won't save him and will only harm you. Tell us what you know about his rebellion."

"I don't know anything! Please, there must be a mistake."

But Emilia knew there wasn't a mistake. She had complete faith in the Order, always had. But watching her father be thrown into that cart...

She could tell them she *thought* she overheard him discussing dragons. *Thought* she heard him say something about the Guardians. But she could be wrong about what she *thought* she heard. Right? Her

Chapter 3

doubt was enough to keep her from incriminating him. It wasn't lying if she wasn't sure. Was it?

They asked the same questions in different ways over and over. And every time, Emilia answered the same. *I don't know.* She almost believed herself when they finally led her to the room where her mother waited.

She didn't know anything. She'd been wrong about what she had heard. Her father was going to be okay. It was going to be fine. But then she saw her mother's face and her hope vanished. Silvia's eyes were laced with worry. Her lips were drawn tight with concern.

The door was locked behind Emilia, and she hurried across the room to her mother. Silvia's arms wrapped around her. The tears broke free.

"Shh, my sweet," Silvia whispered. "It's alright."

"It's not alright," Emilia said through tears. "I heard the two of you speaking the other night and Dad said—"

"Not here," Silvia whispered. "Not when they're listening."

Silvia's warning confirmed that Emilia had heard him speak out against the Order. Had her mother also betrayed it? Would she be held accountable? Part of Emilia wanted to rush to the door and confess, but something in her mother's touch held her back.

There wasn't time to dwell on it. The door opened

and two officers stepped inside, holding the door wide. "It's time to go."

"Where?" Silvia asked, arms still around Emilia's shoulders.

"Your husband's trial is about to start."

✦✦✦

Emilia entered one of the courtrooms on the lower level of the Central Tower. She'd never seen the inside. The room was a large square with a raised platform along the front. A broad, mahogany desk paired with an oversized, plush chair covered in wine velvet sat at an angle on the right side of the platform.

Across from the desk was a single wooden chair. Without needing to be told, Emilia knew her father would sit there. The rest of the room held rows of benches, six on either side, a wide aisle running down the center. Two tall, wooden doors capped the aisle end, where Emilia and her mother had just come through. Silvia and Emilia took seats in the second row along the right.

Faces she didn't know filled the courtroom. Emilia wondered who they were. Why they were here? Had they been asked to come? Were they friends or foes? Gawkers, likely, here to witness the betrayal of the

Chapter 3

Order. So, they were foes.

Seven Order Guards stood stationed around the room. Their faces were stern, their belts armed with long swords. The double doors opened behind them, and Emilia turned to see Ruth, the Grand Master, and the Overseer walking through.

Emilia's heart dropped at the sight of her friend, then panicked at the sight of the Overseer, Victoria, who struck fear into any room. She was also dressed in black, a long-sleeved gown her standard attire. The Overseer was the Grand Master's second, an adviser who understood the law of the Order better than anyone.

Emilia wanted to reach out for Ruth as she passed, but the girl didn't raise her eyes. She walked by as if Emilia and Silvia weren't there. Ruth, her father, and the Overseer walked to the platform. Ruth sat in the front row while the Grand Master and the Overseer stepped up on stage. A short, plump man stood up from the first row and stepped forward. Dressed formally, his silver metal band on display, he faced them and spoke.

"All rise for the Grand Master." The gathered stood. The Grand Master walked across the platform toward the desk, the Overseer following, then turned to face the crowd.

A small door to the left of the platform opened, and

two compliance officers escorted her father into the courtroom. Emilia's breath caught as the officers led him onto the stage and toward the empty wooden chair. The room stood in wait, all eyes on the Grand Master. He took a moment to regard Korin, then walked to the wine-colored chair and sat. The Overseer moved to stand slightly behind the chair, and the plump man with the sliver armband spoke again.

"You may be seated."

The room sat, including Emilia's father, who was forced into his chair. It creaked under his weight, and Emilia flinched at the officer's rough handling.

"This court session has been called to deliberate the accused Korin Harker for claims of rebellion against the Order," the Grand Master began. He looked nothing like his daughter except for the bright blue eyes. They said Ruth was a spitting image of her mother, who passed away during childbirth. The same golden curls, same petite frame, same fair skin. Those who knew Ruth's mother best also said her soul lived in the young girl. They shared the same will for life. Ruth didn't talk about her mother much, and Emilia found it strange to think of her now.

Maybe her brain was just trying to cope, distract itself from the horror at hand. But then her mind returned to the courtroom. There was no escape.

Chapter 3

No distractions.

"Will the prosecutor present its claims against the accused?" the Grand Master asked.

The Overseer nodded to the plump man, who was still standing. The prosecutor. He turned to face her father and began.

"The Order, through acquired evidence, testimony, and self-admission, accuses Korin Harker of slander against the Order—"

Whispers coursed through the crowd. Emilia gripped the edge of her bench to still her shaking hands.

"—and association with the rebel group known as the Guardians," the prosecutor continued, "who speak of dragons—"

The crowd's voices drowned out the rest of the man's words. Emilia's blood pumped in her ears.

The Grand Master opened a small drawer in the wide desk and withdrew a small gavel. He repeatedly rapped it against the desk. The voices abruptly stopped, and the Grand Master gave the plump man a nod to continue. The fat man faced her father, and the officers beside him yanked him to his feet.

"Korin Harker," the prosecutor announced. "Having heard the accusations brought against you in this courtroom, how do you answer?"

Her father scanned the room until his eyes found

Emilia's. His expression lightened. Emilia felt tears burning across her vision as her father held her gaze softly. His own eyes misted, and she saw something undecipherable in his expression. Where she expected to see only fear, there was pride. Or maybe it was hope? For a moment, the rest of the courtroom vanished.

Her father had always been a quiet man. Strong, loyal, unwavering. He'd been her safety and shield. She couldn't remember ever thinking he wouldn't be there to guide and protect her. She'd never questioned his love. Her body reacted before her mind could process what might come next, and she felt faint.

He smiled just enough for her to see, then spoke without removing his eyes from her.

"There is more to this world than you know," he said directly to her. "All you accuse me of is true."

A sense of dread dropped into Emilia's gut. Frantic, accusing whispers filled the room, and the Grand Master stood, gavel slamming on the desk.

Emilia couldn't pull her gaze from her father's face. Fear had crept into the corners of his eyes because he knew what his confession would mean.

"Order," the Grand Master demanded. The room quietened. The Grand Master remained standing as silence settled over the room. He seemed deep in thought, and Emilia finally dragged her eyes from her father. She thought maybe empathy flashed across the

Chapter 3

Grand Master's face. But it left quickly, as if it had never been there at all.

"The penalty for these crimes is clear," the Grand Master said. "Korin, for your offense against the Order that we serve, I find you guilty, and sentence you to death by lethal injection tomorrow at dusk." His gavel struck the desk to solidify his words.

The room became a blur as Emilia drew her eyes back to her father. Things were happening around her: voices, maybe her mother's cry. Movement, perhaps the Grand Master making his way down off the platform. But all Emilia saw was her father. His face had paled, and he was trembling. The officers were yanking him backward toward the door, and Emilia was on her feet before she knew her body was moving. She stepped forward but a hand grasped her wrist to hold her back.

Her eyes never left her father. Her brain was trying to memorize every line in his face because it realized the truth ahead of her heart. She wasn't going to see him ever again. Tears drained down her cheeks as her father vanished through the door.

A gentle tug on her wrist brought her back to the courtroom, which had quietened.

The Grand Master, the man who had just sentenced her father to death, reached out to touch Ruth's shoulder.

"Heartache makes us stronger," the Grand Master

said to her. "Thank you for bringing these crimes to our attention." He removed his hand and left without another word as confusion swarmed Emilia. She found Ruth's watery gaze. Guilt, profound and unmistakable, filled her best friend's eyes.

Truth slammed into Emilia.

She had told Ruth about her father.

And Ruth had told the Grand Master.

CHAPTER 4

VICTORIA, Overseer of all that was sacred, sat in the Grand Master's private office and watched the man pour himself a dark drink. Just past him stood a large, arched window, the sun casting deep hues of orange across the sky as it sank below the mountains.

But an hour ago, the trial of Korin Harker had ended, and still, the moment gnawed at Victoria's mind like a termite at wood. The sentencing was just. She felt no reservations about that. The accused's final statement to his young daughter made her uneasy, though.

There is more to this world than you know.

The words were almost hopeful. Which made them dangerous. Victoria crossed her knees and placed her hands in her lap. Her pale skin contrasted with her black dress in the shadows of Martin's study. She preferred to keep her face clear and had her midnight hair gathered and twisted into a thick, braided bun at the nape of her swanlike neck. The hairstyle showed off the severity of her jaw and expression.

In all things be vigilant. In all things be true. This mantra of the Overseers had been passed down through the generations. She knew better than anyone why the Overseers existed, why their path must be maintained.

The Order ruled with strict laws and punishment, which invoked fear. Fear was her most powerful weapon. Humanity had destroyed itself twice before the warlord Sylas had formed the Order. Now the office of Overseer ensured humanity would never destroy itself again, and it did so through fear. Her mother used to say, "It is better the be afraid than to be dead."

But the Grand Master was prone to weakness.

Victoria knew Martin felt a stab of guilt over the Korin Harker ruling. The Harker family was close to the Grand Master's family. Korin had taught Ruth to ride horses and tended to the Grand Master's personal stable.

Martin was weak, but he was also a true believer and easy to steer in the right direction. For that, she was grateful. But he relied on his feelings more than she'd like. Emotions of guilt and shame had no place inside a king. The law was all that mattered.

Chapter 4

Martin turned to her, his face in shadow as light faded from the sky. A flash of conflict crossed his eyes and Victoria thought he might say something, but a soft rap at the study door kept his words at bay.

"Come," Martin said.

The door opened and Ruth entered. An irritated flare rushed through Victoria. As a young Overseer, just thirty, it was likely that one day she would advise Ruth. The child was worse than her father, and Victoria was not looking forward to her rule. She remained in her seat as the girl approached the center of the room.

Ruth's eyes were red and swollen, her face blotchy. She'd been crying, which didn't surprise Victoria in the least. Victoria turned her gaze back to Martin and saw compassion settle over his face.

"Father, I . . ." Ruth started, then faltered.

Martin exhaled softly. "Hard decisions have to be made."

"But what if I was wrong?" Ruth's voice was hardly more than a whisper.

"You weren't," Victoria stated. "He confessed."

"You were right to confide in me," Martin told Ruth. "I'm proud of you, daughter."

Ruth shook her head slightly. "What if Emilia never forgives me?" Another tear slid down the girl's cheeks.

"Emilia will see reason," Martin said. "She

understands the law. She has always been faithful. Despite this pain, she'll know what you did was right."

"I feel like I betrayed her," Ruth whispered.

"You stood for the Order," Martin said. "In that, there can be no fault." He placed his hand on her small shoulder. "You did the right thing."

Ruth swallowed and sniffed. She nodded and used the heel of her hand to wipe the tears from her cheeks.

"You should rest," Martin said. "I'll have food brought to your room. Go."

The girl stole a final look up at her father and then left. Victoria and Martin fell into silence for a moment. After several long seconds, Martin exhaled heavily and rubbed his temple with his free hand, his crystal tumbler still clutched in the other.

"I hate to see her in pain," Martin said.

"Better this than the pain she would experience if rebellion took hold," Victoria countered.

"Of course," Martin sighed, "but I still wish I could save her from it."

"Soon, *she* will be making these choices. And she'll have to put her feelings aside, as you do."

Martin turned to her. "Do you feel nothing?" His voice wasn't condescending or cruel. In fact, she didn't miss the slight teasing. His gaze lingered on her a moment longer than it should. His longing flickered

Chapter 4

momentarily. Come and then gone, like a flash of lightning. Victoria knew his feelings for her had shifted over time. He was fond of her in an inappropriate way for their working relationship. He was the Grand Master, after all, and she was the Overseer. Certain things were forbidden.

But that didn't stop his desire. Martin would never act on it; she was confident of that. And grateful. She often wondered if maybe she was fond of him too. But she silenced any and all feelings as quickly as they rose. There could be no space in her heart for him. Her heart belonged to another. But she wouldn't hesitate to use his feelings to her advantage.

"Of course, I feel," Victoria said, leaning back and letting her arms grace the armrests of her chair. "But only when it serves the law of the Order."

Martin huffed and tossed back the contents of his tumbler. He walked to his desk and set down the empty glass. "Ever the stoic servant. I'm grateful for your consistency in such matters."

"I'm not a mother, but I can empathize with your situation," she said, choosing her words carefully. What came next would be difficult. "However, we need to discuss the Harker family."

"Silvia and Emilia were questioned," Martin said. "I've known them my whole life. Silvia is my most treasured seamstress. Emilia is Ruth's closest companion."

"I know the situation is difficult, Grand Master, but they shared a home with the accused. And Silvia's interrogation was questionable. I believe they know more than they're saying, and that's dangerous for the Order. If they talk, belief in the prophecy could spread like wildfire."

"The prophecy is no real threat," Martin said, facing her. "The rebels have spoken about a golden egg and the return of dragons for over a hundred years. But we've never been able to locate the egg. It's a myth. It doesn't exist. I assure you that the desert rebels, these Guardians, don't know where it is either. The prophecy is a tale of children."

"But Korin did speak about dragons—he admitted this. So, their belief is real. And belief is enough to be a threat."

Martin placed his hands inside his pockets and turned his eyes to the floor. His tall frame cast a broad shadow on the ground. His dark hair, maintained neatly as always, and warm complexion, glowed in the light of the desk lamp. Victoria couldn't deny his physical appeal, the kindness of his blue eyes, the attraction of his smile. He drew admiring looks from many women. But his eyes were often trained toward her.

Chapter 4

Victoria stood; her lean figure draped to perfection in her black attire. "An idea, like a seed, can grow with little attention. Before you realize it, it's started to take root. Think of what he said to his daughter."

Martin drew his eyes to her face as Victoria crossed to the opposite end of the desk, keeping half a dozen feet between them. She would never touch him out of turn. Her presence this close was strong enough.

"Think of Ruth," Victoria said softly. "She spends hours with Emilia. Confides in her. We must protect the future of the Order."

"What are you proposing?" Martin asked.

"That Silvia and Emilia be put on trial, so we ensure this bout of rebellion is silenced."

Victoria could see the disturbance in his eyes.

"Ruth would be crushed!" he said.

"Better to be crushed by heartbreak than poisoned by heretics. We cannot, under any circumstances, allow the seed of doubt and rebellion to thrive. Your own daughter's rule depends on it. Do it, for Ruth's well-being. For her survival."

He held her gaze for another moment and then paced, hands clasped behind his back. Victoria waited, knowing she'd already won.

He finally turned to face her. He said nothing, just gave a nod.

She returned the gesture. "I'll see it's done before I leave for the New Moon Ceremony in two days."

"Is it time for that again?" he said with an attempt at lightheartedness, but she could hear the heaviness in his voice.

"An age-old tradition of the Overseer's I'd never think to forgo," Victoria said.

"No, of course not. I'll speak with Ruth in the morning."

"Very well. Do you require anything else, Grand Master?"

He held her gaze for another long moment and again, something stirred behind his eyes. But he only cleared his throat and shook his head.

"Then I'll take my leave," Victoria said. She walked to the study door, leaving the man staring in her wake.

✦✦✦

Emilia could hardly feel her body as she lay in bed. Maybe it was protecting her from the pain she should be feeling in her chest. The ache that should be threatening to collapse her heart. Instead, she'd gone numb.

The sun was gone. How long had she been home since the trial? An hour? Several? She'd lost sense of time. Emilia didn't remember the journey home; she

Chapter 4

just knew her mother had pulled her from the courtroom and now she was here in her bed.

The world came crashing in all at once. They were going to kill her father. The weight of it was crushing her bones. She struggled to breathe. To think. She'd been going through this cycle since the Grand Master decided her father's fate.

From feeling nothing to feeling every nerve ending. From numbness to crushing pain.

This is your fault.

Your fault.

Your fault.

The shame and guilt capsized her. She sank below the icy waters of regret. She'd done this. And now her father would die because of her.

Something stirred outside her shut bedroom door. Steps paired with rustling movements. Emilia managed to push herself up. Her arms shook. Nausea rolled through her stomach. Tears dripped past her lips, the salty taste reminding her she'd started crying again.

Or maybe she'd never stopped.

Emilia stood and left her bedroom. The main room beyond was dark but for the single light in the kitchen and the roar of the fire. Her mother moved about with intentional steps. Quick and focused. A small suitcase sat open on the couch; items stuffed inside.

Blankets.

Clothes.

Books.

Not much. They didn't have much. Emilia didn't recognize the cardboard box beside the fire. Her mother stood over it, pulling out books and tearing out pages before throwing them into the fire. Her father's journals.

Emilia rushed across the room and yanked one of the journals from her mother's hands without thinking. "Don't," she yelled. "These were his."

Surprised, Silvia turned to Emilia as if she hadn't realized the girl was there. She yanked the leather book back, sympathy and tears mingled in her eyes.

"I know, but he wrote things . . ." She tossed the whole book into the fire. Emilia moved to save it, but her mother grabbed hold of her wrist.

"I need you to listen to me," Silvia said.

"I'm so sorry," Emilia blurted out. "I did this. I did this and I'm so sorry."

Silvia's hold of Emilia's wrist eased, and she pulled her daughter against her chest. "No, no, you *didn't* do this."

Emilia cried hard enough to shake her shoulders as her mother pulled her tighter. Her heart was cracking with each sob.

Chapter 4

"I was foolish and naïve," Emilia sobbed. "I never should have said anything to anyone."

"No, Emilia," Silvia whispered, pulling away from her daughter and cupping her face. "You're not to blame. You hear me? This isn't your doing. It's theirs."

Emilia sniffed as tears rolled off her chin. She shook her head, and her mother began wiping her tears away with her thumbs.

"They did this. The Order is responsible. Not you."

Emilia opened her mouth to tell her mother she'd never forgive herself for what she'd done, but only a sob croaked out.

"We aren't safe here anymore," Silvia continued. "We have to hide any evidence against your father and go." Silvia returned to the box and yanked out a worn, yellowed item along with a small token Emilia had never seen. Silvia placed them both in the long side pocket of her gray cotton skirt, like the one she'd sewn for Emilia, then tossed what remained from the box into the flames.

"We have to leave."

Emilia's mind spun. "What? Leave, we can't—"

"We must. They will come for us, and I will not let you suffer the same fate as your father."

"I don't understand," Emilia said.

That stilled her mother for a moment. Silvia let out

a long slow breath. She gently took Emilia's hands.

"Over four months ago, your father received a letter from his brother," Silvia said.

"Brother? I didn't know he had a brother."

"He vanished over twenty years ago. Rumors of him running off to join the Guardians circled through the community like wildfire. It was best for your grandparents and father to distance themselves from him. So, they vowed to never speak of him. But your father thought of him often. I could always tell when he was lost in thoughts of him."

Silvia took another deep breath. "So, when a letter from him showed up, your father couldn't ignore it, even after all that time. Your uncle's name is Luca. He told your father he was dying. He wanted to make peace with your father and asked that he meet him in the Wastelands, outside Capital City."

"He went?"

Silvia nodded. "He tried not to. But the yearning to make peace with his brother and see him again before the end . . . you know how fiercely loyal your father is. He went and learned that Luca had been with the Guardians. I don't know everything they discussed; I just know that meeting changed everything in the man I love. He came back different."

Her mother stared at the fire. "I begged him to forget

Chapter 4

it. To leave it alone, but..." A short laugh mingled with a sob escaped her throat, and Emilia's chest tightened. Silvia dropped her daughter's hands and stepped back, then ran her fingers through her raven hair and closed her eyes, tears sneaking through the corners.

"Mom..."

A knock at the door stopped her cold. Silvia's eyes snapped open. She put a finger to her lips to command Emilia's silence, then crept to the front door as the knock sounded again. Silvia stole a glance through the window, trying to keep her body hidden along the wall, then cast Emilia a questioning look.

She reached for the knob and opened the door. Ruth stood on the front step, draped in a hooded, woolen shawl that hung to her calves. The girl stepped through, and Silvia closed the door.

"Ruth?" Emilia whispered.

Ruth yanked off her hood and looked from Emilia to Silvia. Her mouth was a tight line, and her fingers were shaking. Ruth's eyes filled with tears.

"I . . . I'm sorry to come so late," Ruth said.

"Did your father send you?" Silvia asked. "Are your guards with you?"

"No," Ruth quickly answered. "I came alone. After . . ." She didn't need to say more.

"Why are you here?" Emilia asked. She couldn't stop

the anger that heated her face.

"I came to warn you," Ruth answered. "Victoria, the Overseer," she said with a shake of her head. "She convinced the Grand Master to put you both on trial."

"How do you know this?" Silvia asked as Emilia's mouth gaped.

"I overheard them in my father's study this evening. I came as soon as I realized he was going to agree."

"But we haven't done anything," Emilia said.

More tears glistened in Ruth's eyes, the fire illuminating the moisture on her cheeks. "That won't matter. I don't think it's safe for you here anymore."

A beat of silence filled the room.

"You came here alone to warn us?" Emilia asked, emotions caught in her throat.

"Of course I came. I was a terrible friend to you once. I wasn't about to be again."

Something in Emilia broke and she found herself rushing forward and crushing Ruth in a hug. Both girls cried for a moment before either spoke.

"I'm so sorry," Ruth squeaked.

Silvia reached up and touched Emilia's shoulder. "We need to go."

Her face awash with tears, Emilia pulled back from Ruth. Emilia didn't know what to say. She stepped back as Ruth pulled Emilia's cloak from a nearby hook and

Chapter 4

handed it to her. Silvia rushed across the room, stuffed a last item into the suitcase, and grabbed a burlap bag from the kitchen countertop.

Emilia took the shoulder bag from her mother as Silvia turned to Ruth. "Thank you," she whispered and placed a kiss atop the girl's head. Then she yanked Emilia toward the front door.

Emilia turned back only once to share a final look with Ruth. They shared no good-byes or wishes for good luck. Just a knowing look that felt like a promise. They would see each other again.

Silvia yanked her daughter into the night and away from the only life she'd ever known.

CHAPTER 5

EMILIA FOLLOWED SILVIA through the city toward the closest stable. They needed a horse and fast. The night was bitterly cold and the stars were nowhere to be seen. Storm clouds hung overhead, and Emilia prayed they wouldn't open and pour down. She'd opened her mouth once to ask her mother where they would go. but Silvia silenced her with a finger to her lips. Emilia hadn't dared speak again.

They moved so quickly that her legs started to burn. She kept her eyes focused on her feet and surroundings. She knew they were headed toward Second Ring. No one in Third Ring had personal stables, and to steal a horse from a community stable would be too risky. There was too much foot traffic at that hour, too many possible encounters. The closest community stable to their home in Third Ring held over a hundred and fifty horses.

The Golden Egg

A private stable held maybe two or three horses, five for the most elite, but all were in First Ring, and there was no need to travel that far. With Emilia's father working in the Central Tower's main stable, she'd spent hours among the beautiful creatures. She'd only ridden a dozen times but watched Ruth learn to ride her own horse, Freckle, elegantly.

If she ever owned a horse, she'd want a blonde mare with white-haired hooves and golden eyes. She'd name it Caramel or Butterscotch, which reminded her of candy and summer.

Silvia darted into a small stone alcove, snapping Emilia's focus back to attention. Emilia nearly stumbled as she twisted to follow and scooted into the darkened overhang.

Her mother peered out to survey the way ahead. They were in Second Ring near the outer edge, behind a double-storied home with white, wooden paneling and a half dozen dark windows. A green lawn stretched about twenty yards from their alcove to the back patio.

The stone archway where they hid looked like part of a gazebo of some sort. Emilia wondered what it would be like to have enough wealth to build an extra structure in the backyard. Or to have a backyard in the first place.

The gazebo sat in the back corner of the yard. In

Chapter 5

the opposite corner was a small stable. She heard a soft neigh from the creature housed inside. Silvia turned and mouthed for Emilia to *stay put,* then darted into the night toward the stable.

Emilia wanted to reach out for her mother. What if she was caught? What was Emilia supposed to do then? Stealing was a great offense. She trusted the Order, but she was running from them. They hadn't done anything wrong, but that wouldn't be true if they stole this horse. The Order had sentenced her father to die, but Emilia still yearned for its promise of safety.

She shivered and yanked her humble coat tighter across her chest. Minutes ticked by and she held her breath. Dread filled her gut and terror filled her bones.

She heard her mother before her eyes could make out her shape. Silvia came into focus out of the dead of night, a gentle horse in tow, and Emilia released the breath she'd been holding. Her mother motioned for her to follow, and Emilia slipped from the alcove. She moved around the corner and down the slight hill that spread out into a small field. Emilia followed until they were tucked in a thicket of trees and Silvia stopped. She brushed the horse's nose and took a moment to whisper to the animal, offering it comfort.

"What now?" Emilia asked.

"We ride for the Wastelands," Silvia said.

Emilia sucked in a terrified breath. Nothing good was to be found in the Wastelands. But she said nothing as they climbed onto the steed and set off.

✦✦✦

Silvia and Emilia wove through the Capital City, staying in the shadows and alleyways as they traveled toward Capital City's south exit. Only two main roads led through the city's outskirts and toward the Wastelands.

What waited for them there? Emilia didn't know and her mother didn't give her answers. She was too focused on getting them out of the city. So, Emilia's imagination ran wild to stories of monsters and sandstorms and grueling sun. People who entered the Wastelands didn't return. Ruth often repeated a story she'd heard from a guard about a band of desert people called Marauders who stole wanderers' belongings, stripped them naked, and left them for dead on the dry sands.

But that probably wasn't true, Emilia thought. Right?

Silvia guided the horse through a dark alleyway as they entered Sixth Ring. Emilia had watched the evidence of wealth and privilege decay in each ring.

Chapter 5

Here, roads became dirt paths and muddy walkways. The homes were broken and frail, stacked end to end in places. Voices echoed into the night as people argued, babies cried, and mothers begged for sleep. All their walls were too thin to offer privacy.

People wandered the streets, looking for an escape from their troubles. Some walked into dens of sin that offered drinks to help numb reality. Others begged for money or help. Life was grim here in Sixth Ring. There was no peace, no comfort. Every passing glance brought a shiver to Emilia's skin. A man with missing teeth caught her eye and offered her a smile that wasn't friendly but rather hungry. Emilia tore her gaze away and held tighter to her mother's waist.

With the sheer number of people, Emilia had always imagined that the streets of Sixth Ring would be overrun with compliance officers, but she was shocked they hadn't seen one. She supposed she should feel lucky. Would the Order know they had run by now? Were compliance officers looking for them?

Emilia wondered for the hundredth time if they were making a terrible mistake. Maybe Ruth's warning had been in vain. They could have gone to the Grand Master. Maybe worked out an understanding. As if in response to her thoughts, Silvia's body went rigid.

Emilia looked around her mother's shoulder to

see three compliance officers on horseback, red bands around their forearms, riding in their direction. Silvia yanked the reins and steered their mount down an alley to the left. Emilia could feel her mother's heart pounding as she softly kicked the horse with her heels to quicken its pace.

For a moment, Emilia relaxed, but then the sound of another horse behind them reignited her fear. She craned her neck to see the compliance officers had turned to follow them. They were one hundred yards behind but following at a leisurely pace.

"Hold on," Silvia said, then snapped the reins. The horse charged as Emilia clung to her mother's waist. Voices shouted, and Emilia knew without looking that the officers were calling for them to stop. Their horse's hooves pounded across the muddy street as Silvia drove the steed as fast as she could away from the threat.

The wind slapped Emilia's cheeks and dried her throat as they rounded a corner and tore through a couple walking. The innocent passersby screamed and launched themselves out of the way as Silvia pressed forward. A group of men stumbled out of a very loud home, visibly swaying, and were nearly trampled by the horse's thundering hooves.

Citizens' shouts now mixed with the compliance

Chapter 5

officers', swirling around Emilia's head.

"Yaw!" Silvia yelled as she snapped the reins, begging the creature to move. She made a quick turn right and then another left. A final right took them beyond the homes into desert lands. The scenery blurred with their pace. The homes disappeared and only the sparse desert foliage and rolling sands surrounded them.

They raced up a small dune and then down the opposite side, and a thick stand of trees appeared to their left. Something sailed through the air and struck the sand to Emilia's right. An arrow. The compliance officers were shooting at them!

"Stop in the name of the Order!" a voice cried.

Their horse drove into the thicket and a branch caught Emilia's shoulder, ripping a slash in her sleeve. No more voices came. No more arrows sailed toward them. Still, Silvia pressed on, the horse twisting and turning through the brush. Emilia shifted and saw the way behind them was clear though she could still hear the distant sound of pursuit.

Several quiet minutes passed with only the sound of their horse's thudding hooves. Panting, her mother steered the mount toward something ahead.

She pulled to a stop.

"What are you doing?" Emilia asked.

"Hiding you," Silvia answered. She jumped from

the horse and helped Emilia off, then directed her to a shallow, craggy rock overhang. "Get underneath," her mother ordered. Emilia hesitated, terror revealing her mother's intention.

"We won't both fit in there," Emilia said.

Her mother looked to make sure the coast was still clear. When she turned back to Emilia, her eyes were filled with sadness. "I know."

"No . . ." Emilia started.

Silvia grabbed her daughter's shoulders and held her eyes. "I'll draw them away, make sure I lose them completely, and then I'll be back."

"No." Emotion threatened to steal Emilia's voice.

"It's the only way," Silvia said. She placed a hand against Emilia's right cheek. "I will not let them take you from me too. Now . . ." She grabbed the burlap shoulder bag and handed it to Emilia. "Take this. There's some food and water inside. Just enough. And this." She dug the yellowed parchment and token from her skirt pocket. The things Emilia had seen her take from her father's box.

"If anything happens to me, follow this map. It will lead you to the Guardians. Give them this token and tell them your uncle was Luca Harker and you're looking for safety."

"Mom, I—"

Chapter 5

"Don't fight me on this! Not this, Emilia. If I'm not back in an hour, you must find your way to them. They will protect you until I can come for you."

Emilia was shaking her head, but her mother ushered her toward the hiding place. Silvia yanked Emilia into a fierce embrace and placed a hot kiss against her cheek. "I love you, my sweet girl."

With a nod, her mother turned to go. Emilia reached for her a final time, grasping the hem of her skirt the way she had done a thousand times as a child. Silvia offered a brave smile. "Stay hidden," she said, then disappeared into the night.

A moment later, Emilia heard the horse's hooves pounding against the packed sand, moving away, fading quickly, leaving her in total silence. Emilia listened, straining to hear anything as she lay there. Her heart pounded in her ears. Her breath was short and hot.

There was nothing she could do now except wait as her mother had instructed. An hour, she'd said. But how long was an hour? Every minute felt like an hour.

Emilia didn't know how long she lay there, curled up under the overhang, her muscles begging for release. Eventually, she eased herself from the alcove and peered out into the desert. The still brush and sand were all she saw. She stepped further into the open air, careful as she stood straight. Again, she listened for any threat. For her mother. But nothing came. Fear pulsed under her skin.

She was totally alone. Now what?

She should probably return to the hiding place and wait longer. But surely more than an hour had passed. Emilia saw something long and dark slither beneath the craggy rock. She bit down on her tongue to silence her scream as every inch of her skin crawled. There was no way she was going back in there.

Panic enveloped her like a thick fog. She should have stayed in her hideaway and let the slithering monster eat her. Anxiety smothered her senses. She was just a girl. What did her mother expect her to do?

Two paths made themselves apparent. Emilia could lie down and wait for something to happen to her, and wallow in her fear and pain—a choice that felt overwhelmingly strong. Or she could try to find her way through the Wastelands. That would require a bravery she wasn't sure she possessed. Emilia closed her eyes, and a vision of Ruth filled her mind. Ruth would press on.

She opened her eyes, took several deep breaths, and, with shaky fingers, yanked the yellowed parchment from the burlap bag. After unfolding the map, she stared at its lines, just visible in the moonlight. It was

Chapter 5

simple and hand-drawn. There was Capital City, clearly marked, and the desert that stretched out from the city's boundaries, a small forest that might be the one she was in now, a wide expanse of desert sand, and then a mountain range directly south with a small lake at its base. A direct path to the mountains had been laid out.

She had to head south, then.

Her father had loved the stars. He'd read her ancient stories about a time when humans had traveled to the stars and walked on the moon, which felt like it couldn't be true. There were planets and constellations, an entire galaxy of wonders and possibilities. It had always captured Emilia's attention and made her giggle with excitement.

She knew the stars enough to look for the North Star. Sitting at the tail end of the Little Dipper, it would show her north. She found the constellations with ease and spotted true north. At least she hoped that was true north.

She put it at her back and walked south, hoping all her father had taught her was correct. She walked through the thicket of desert trees, past more rigid rock formations, and finally into the dunes.

Emilia slogged for hours, walking until her legs felt like rubber and her heart ached from the exertion. She lifted the water her mother had given her and tried to drink it with shaky hands. But she only managed one swig before she tripped over a rock. The canteen fell from her grasp and dumped its precious contents, quickly soaking the sand. Her spirits fell as the water disappeared, leaving barely a swallow in the bottom of the canteen.

As the last of her hopes also slipped away, Emilia could think of no better option than to move forward. So, she did. She walked until the sky turned from black to deep blue and the stars began to fade with the early dawn.

Exhausted, Emilia collapsed at the base of a lone tree, her body begging for relief. She placed her head against its trunk as her chest labored to breathe. Her throat burned and the silence gnawed at her. She tried to control the emotion collecting around her heart, but it was too much.

More tears filled her eyes and she crumpled to her side, dragging her knees toward her chin. She was waterless. Fatherless. Motherless.

Alone.

She wept until fatigue drew her into a deep sleep.

CHAPTER 6

SILVIA'S EYES SNAPPED OPEN, and a cloudy breath left her lungs. The scene around her was dark and cold. Her skin felt heavy with moisture, the air damp. For a moment, she couldn't remember where she was. And then a flash of awareness sparked, and memories roared to life like flames.

Ruth showing up to warn them.

Stealing a horse from Second Ring.

Almost making it out. Being pursued.

Leaving Emilia in the Wasteland.

Being apprehended and dragged back to First Ring.

Thrown in a cell.

Imprisoned.

Silvia pushed herself up from the narrow stone bench, where sleep had finally come in the early morning hours. Her resistant muscles screamed. Every tendon was sore from exertion. Her head pounded from lack of sleep and water. Her chest ached from the ramped emotions.

She had held no illusions about returning to Emilia. Silvia knew she couldn't escape the pursuit of the officers; that was the reason she'd hidden Emilia in the first place. Still, the moment they had rounded on her, terror seized her body. They'd dragged her back to the Central Tower and deep into its underbelly where the dungeons were built.

Had that just been last night? Was it morning now? It was impossible to tell time in the dark, windowless cell. Silvia wondered if Korin was close. Ice filled her chest. Or maybe he was already dead. The Grand Master's voice flittered through her brain.

I find you guilty and sentence you to death by lethal injection tomorrow at dusk.

Silvia pressed back against the wall, bringing her knees up to her chest. She laid her forehead against them as rolling emotions crushed her. Fear, loss, shame, regret, anger. The onslaught of feelings came in waves that threatened to drown her. She'd held them off while her focus was on saving Emilia. Mothers did that. Tampered with their feelings to attend to their children. Silvia had been singularly focused on ensuring Emilia was safe. But now she was gone and there was nothing

Chapter 6

but Silvia's self-control to keep her heartache at bay.

She was too weak now. Like the pages of a children's storybook—the kind Emilia had learned to read while sitting on their living room floor—images from Silvia's life flipped through her mind. She'd loved Korin Harker from the moment she saw him. She was a sixteen-year-old girl, still living in her parents' home, and he an eighteen-year-old boy with long limbs and a quiet demeanor. He worked with his father in the royal stables and she studied under tailoring her own father. They didn't speak those first few years. Silvia was nearly eighteen by the time Korin worked up the courage to talk to her.

But she already knew she loved him. She'd just been waiting for him to catch up. They married a year later, young but so, so happy. He was warm and sound and sure. He made their home sturdy and safe. Korin was the calm in the storm of her wild emotions. She used to get angry with him for that. She wanted him to react, but he didn't. It was as if he saw Silvia held enough feelings for them both.

Her small laugh turned into a sob and echoed in the dark cell. Her laugh, her sob. Silvia would give anything to feel his calm now. She'd loved the man he'd become after Emilia's birth. Their tiny, perfect baby had lit a fire in him, a determination to ensure the world was perfect for his child.

The ache in Silvia's heart expanded as she thought of her daughter. Had Emilia heeded Silvia's words? Would she survive the Wastelands? Maybe the compliance officers had already found her. Losing her husband had broken her heart, but losing her daughter... That would destroy her completely.

Silvia took a breath through her tears and lifted her head. She sat upright and focused her mind. *No*, she thought. *Emilia is strong and capable. I have to believe she will find the Guardians and be safe.*

Something squeaked outside her cell door, and Silvia held her breath. She couldn't see much. Only a few dim lights hung every few yards, illuminating the prison. Footsteps approached, and she waited to see the figure appear.

Two breaths later, the shadows shifted, and three bodies approached her cell. Through the bars, Silvia could tell two were built like trucks and had dark red bands on their forearms. Compliance officers. The third was smaller, but no less dangerous.

The Overseer.

✦ ✦ ✦

The previous night had not gone as expected. Victoria

Chapter 6

had thought the collection of Silvia and Emilia Harker would be simple, so arriving at their home and finding they'd fled had complicated her evening. Upon receiving the news, she'd sent compliance officers and the city guard toward the Capital City borders in all directions. Victoria assumed the Harkers would seek out the Guardians, hoping to find refuge with the rebels. That's what she would have done in their shoes.

They'd been discovered heading south, which was interesting. For over a hundred and fifty years, the Order and the Overseers had searched for the Guardians to no avail. The heretics, small in number and excellent at hiding their tracks, had been a problem without resolution for far too long. Their belief in a golden dragon that might rise and redeem them from the oppression of the Order had poisoned many minds.

The belief was based in truth, of course. A golden dragon might hatch one day, which was why the Overseers had done all in their power to locate the rumored golden egg the heretics worshipped. As the fifth Overseer, she'd done her best to find the egg. But the Order could never even get their hands on anyone who had seen it.

They'd captured a handful of Marauders, another hazardous group of people living far beyond city borders to the south. But Victoria was confident the

Marauders didn't have the egg. In fact, they believed the idea of such a thing was absurd. The Marauders had their own twisted beliefs that had never interfered with the Order, so she left them alone and would continue to until they became a problem—at which time, like the desert heretics, the Marauders would be hunted and eliminated.

They had searched for the egg over a hundred miles in every direction and found nothing. Victoria had all but given up, assuming the egg would never be found.

Until now.

The dank dungeons smelled of mildew as Victoria approached Silvia's cell with two compliance officers. The woman looked haggard but sat with her head held high, feigning confidence. In other circumstances, Victoria might admire Silvia. One of the officers opened Silvia's chamber and Victoria walked in alone.

"Give us a moment," she said to the officers, who nodded and left. They wouldn't go too far, but she wasn't afraid. Victoria could handle herself.

"Hello, Silvia," Victoria said.

Silvia stared at her, silent.

"The compliance officers who chased you last night confirmed there were two riders on your stolen horse," Victoria started. "We know Emilia was with you and you hid her somewhere in the Wastelands. I have a

Chapter 6

hundred Order Guards and compliance officers searching the area, but they're coming up empty-handed."

Something resembling relief flashed through Silvia's eyes. Most might not have noticed, but Victoria had always been incredibly perceptive. Ever since she was a little girl, she'd been able to sense and see things others missed. Her father had called it second sight, as though she was gifted. And maybe her father was correct. But Victoria attributed it to her intelligence. She knew from a young age that being an Overseer was her destiny. Her parents had brought her forth as a contender at the age of five. She'd honed her skills of perception through diligence and practice. It made her a formidable opponent.

"I'm not a mother," Victoria continued, "but I assume you wouldn't send your daughter into the Wastelands without a plan. This leads me to believe you sent her somewhere hoping she would be cared for."

"You don't know me or my daughter," Silvia ground out. Her voice cracked from exhaustion. "Emilia is very resilient."

"Perhaps. But she *is* only thirteen," Victoria said. "And the Wasteland is dangerous for even the most prepared. Regardless, I know you would never give up the location of your daughter. You'd die first. I didn't come here to discuss Emilia."

"Then why tell me?"

"To establish trust."

Silvia huffed.

"I give you something, in this case, the relief that we haven't been able to locate your daughter, and then you give me something."

Silvia observed Victoria carefully. "What do you want?"

"I want to know about the golden dragon egg."

Victoria saw recognition in Silvia's eyes before she could hide it. The woman had heard about the egg, probably from her husband.

"The heretics say a golden dragon will save them from the oppression of the Order," Victoria continued. "What do you know about this?"

"I don't know anything," Silvia lied.

"I know that's not true. I've searched your home. Judging by the pile of ash we found around your fire, you tried to conceal all evidence that might incriminate your husband—and you. However, I did find this."

Victoria pulled the corner of a journal page from her dress pocket, the edge singed and blackened by flame. "Only a few words are legible, but it's enough confirmation. Tell me what you know about the golden egg, Silvia."

"You're lying," Silvia said. "There's probably nothing

Chapter 6

on that scrap."

Victoria offered the partially burned scrap of paper to Silvia. The woman hesitated but took the corner and struggled to control her fear. That was all the confirmation Victoria needed.

It was true then. She noticed a shake start in Silvia's hand and reached to pluck the paper back.

"You should have told me the truth," Victoria said. "I may have shown you and Emilia mercy."

"You'll never find her," Silvia whispered.

"I will," Victoria whispered. "And then you will watch me take her from this world as I take your husband."

Tears rose in Silvia's eyes and the tremble in her fingers moved into her shoulders.

Victoria said nothing else. She turned and calmly left the cell. The door slammed shut behind her as she walked toward the prison's exit. All this time, they'd been searching for the golden egg and the Guardians. Now Victoria knew they were together.

She glanced down at the corner and reread the smudged words.

A Guardian in the desert . . .

Have hope . . .

. . . golden egg.

She spoke over her shoulder. "Keep her locked away

but alive. We may yet need her." The officers nodded as they followed Victoria back up into the light of the new day.

"Send for my horse and my escort," Victoria said. "I leave for the New Moon Ceremony in an hour."

She needed to share what she'd learned with her queen. The Guardians knew where the golden egg was, and Emilia was headed straight for them. Victoria intended to find them both.

CHAPTER 7

SOMETHING JOSTLED Emilia's shoulder. She slowly opened her eyes, light piercing her vision, and a grunt leaving her dry throat. She felt the pounding headache before anything else and wondered why she was lying on the sand and not in her bed.

The next moment was filled with recall, and she sat up quickly. Too quickly.

Ignoring the pain in her bones, she quickly took in her surroundings. The desert floor and a rough tree behind her, its leaves providing splotches of shade across her figure. Tall, thick bunches of cacti several feet away to her left. A jagged rock formation to her right. The mid-afternoon sun blazing down.

And two bodies standing before her. Two men—well, one man and one boy who couldn't be much older than her.

She gasped and scampered back only to hit the scratchy bark of a tree trunk.

The strangers were dressed in lightweight fabrics of desert colors, browns and tans, with most of their skin hidden from the sun. Airy scarves covered their heads and faces, leaving only their eyes visible. Knives of different sizes were strapped to their waists and thighs. They carried packs over their shoulders, and a bow and cluster of arrows in their hands. Emilia heard animals stirring and saw a pair of horses tied to a thicker tree twenty feet away.

Emilia looked from one man to the other, her breaths coming fast and hard. The older of the two yanked his face covering down under his chin and offered a reassuring smile. She must look like a scared animal, because he dropped into a squat and raised his hands.

"It's alright," he said, his voice warm and full. His brown skin contrasted nicely against the linen of his head wrap. His hair was cut short and clean. "We're not going to hurt you."

"Who are you?" Emilia asked.

"My name is Torey, and this is my son, Oliver," the man said. "What's your name?"

She hesitated but knew they couldn't be a part of the Order.

Chapter 7

"Emilia," she said.

Torey continued. "Are you hurt, Emilia?"

"No, I don't think so," she answered.

"Let me help you to your feet," he said, offering a hand. "We have food and water if you need it."

Emilia's fear sparked as she recalled what Ruth had said about Marauders. "You're not"—she started, then bit her lip—"Marauders?"

"Of course not," Oliver huffed. "Be glad those monsters from the south didn't find you."

"They're real?" Emilia asked, her eyes widening.

"Don't they teach you anything in Capital City?" Oliver asked.

His father gave him a stern look and then smiled at Emilia. "We mean you no harm, Emilia. Please let me help you."

His green eyes held nothing but kindness, which could be a trap, but something in her felt like it wasn't. Emilia nodded and took his hand. He helped her to her feet. It hurt to move, and she was grateful for his strength. He reminded her of her father, but she shoved that painful memory away.

Torey motioned to Oliver, who took off his pack and retrieved a canteen from inside. Torey took the canteen, twisted the cap off, and handed it to Emilia. The water felt like heaven on her tongue, cold and sweet, and it slipped down her throat like silk. Surely, they wouldn't offer her water if they were going to kill her. Right?

Torey also offered a short stack of what looked like crackers as she returned the water.

"You need to eat," he said.

"Thank you," she said, sniffing the food. It smelled fresh and like bread, so she took a bite. It tasted like bread too.

"How did you know I was from Capital City?" she said, chewing.

"Look at the way you're dressed," Oliver said. "And there aren't very many places you could be from. If we hadn't been out this far collecting Barra fruit, you'd be in real trouble. What are you doing out here?" Oliver asked.

Barra fruit was rare and only grew twice a year on cacti throughout the desert. So, they were harvesting it? What would have happened to her if they hadn't been this far out? The thought made her shiver.

"Oli," his father said softly.

"It's a fair question," Oliver responded. "Out here all alone, and you can't be more than twelve."

"I'm thirteen, actually," Emilia fired back. "And I didn't start alone." She fought to keep the frailness from her voice, but it was difficult. Because she *was* alone,

Chapter 7

and the weight of her predicament made her feel not only frail but broken.

"You have to forgive Oliver," Torey started. "He's passionate and protective of us."

She looked at the boy. He pulled down his head wrap so she could see his face. He was slightly taller than her, and his dark hair with thick curls and wild strays glistened in the sunshine. Other than the head full of curls, he was a younger replica of his father, with green eyes and warm brown skin.

"You're Guardians?" she said, suddenly thinking it was the only thing that made any sense.

Neither of them said anything, which was practically an admission.

"I was sent to find you," Emilia continued.

"Sent by whom?" Torey asked.

"My mother," Emilia said. "She was with me."

"Where is she now?" Torey asked.

"Taken by compliance officers," Emilia said.

"Compliance officers?" Oliver questioned.

"Don't they teach you anything in the desert?" she snapped without thinking.

Oliver looked taken aback for a moment, then his eyes sparked with something she couldn't quite read, and she watched the corner of his mouth lift into half a grin.

"Compliance officers patrol Capital City throughout the six rings," Emilia answered Oliver's question even though she refused to look at him.

"Why did these compliance officers take your mother?" Torey asked.

"Because my father was recently found guilty of an offense against the Order," Emilia said. "We were next."

"You're a rebel?" Oliver asked, his eyes sparkling with excitement.

"No," she answered. "No, I would never . . . but it doesn't matter. I'm my father's daughter and he . . ." She remembered the wooden token in her knapsack still sitting by the tree. She rushed for it and yanked the bag open. Fishing around with her fingers, she grazed the round edge and pulled it free. She held the token up for them to see.

"My father received this from his brother, Luca Harker," Emilia said.

"You're a Harker?" Torey said.

She nodded. "My father was Korin Harker."

Oliver approached her and held out his hand. Emilia placed the token in his palm and pulled back, careful not to touch him. She didn't know why he made her insides so jittery. He was just a boy.

Oliver examined the token and handed it to his father, who did the same.

Chapter 7

"This is indeed one of ours," Torey said.

"What does it mean?" Emilia asked.

"Each Guardian family is given a token, a symbol of our community," Oliver said. "Luca never married, so he must have given this to his brother."

Torey held the disc to his closed lips. With his eyes shut, he whispered something Emilia couldn't make out and then moved the token from his mouth to his forehead, then heart.

"Luca was a brilliant man," Torey said. "Our community mourns the loss of him still."

"I didn't know him," Emilia said. "I didn't even know I had an uncle until yesterday."

Torey shared a sad smile and returned the token to her. Oliver stayed his father's wrist. "That should go to Clara."

"It's Emilia's," Torey said. "She was in his bloodline."

"What did you do to it?" Emilia asked.

"I thanked my old friend for his love and rejoiced in his final resting glory, for I know I will see him again," Torey answered.

His words were beautiful and stirred something in her gut. Emilia reached out and took the token.

"We should move. We've been out here in the light for too long," Torey said.

"What about me?" Emilia asked.

The Golden Egg

Torey returned to where he had laid his pack and hoisted it over his shoulders. "You'll come with us."

"No," Emilia said.

"Didn't you come looking for us?" Torey asked Emilia.

"Yes . . . but I . . ."

"She's an outsider, Father," Oliver said. "Bastien won't like it."

"You would have us leave her out here alone?" Torey asked. He placed his hand on his son's shoulder. "She goes with us."

Emilia stood there, frozen by indecision. She couldn't return to Capital City, even though every fiber of her being missed home. Her mother wouldn't come for her now, and she couldn't very well storm the city and try to rescue her. Not alone. Maybe she could convince the Guardians to help her. But the thought of turning her back on all she believed by following the Guardians to their rebel camp made her head spin.

Her father had lost his life because of these people.

Even if they had offered her water and kindness . . . even if her mother had sent her to find them . . . it all felt . . . wrong. But what else was she supposed to do? Torey was right. She couldn't stay out here alone. She was out of water and had very little food. The desert would kill her if something else didn't first.

Chapter 7

Oliver was looking at her when she glanced up.

"It has to be your choice," he said.

There was only one reason left to return to the city—her mother. She prayed Mother was okay. She would go with the Guardians and do everything she could to convince them to help her save her mother. Only a few days ago, Ruth had held Emilia's hand and worried that the future would change everything. How unexpectedly quickly that future had come.

Emilia nodded and swung her bag over her shoulder. Without another word, Oliver started for the horses. Torey and Emilia followed closely behind.

✦ ✦ ✦

Emilia rode on the back of Torey's horse as they traveled across the sand, stopping at a small cave just big enough for the three of them and the two horses. Torey told Emilia to rest, as they would be traveling through the night. When Emilia asked why they didn't travel during the day, Torey told her the night offered protection from sight.

Emilia learned the Guardians had existed for a hundred and fifty years, just as long as the Order. Traveling and hunting by night was one of the reasons why they had never been found. Oliver and his father were hunters and they'd been on the tail end of a week-long expedition to find a special fruit when they came across Emilia. They had two or three days of travel to reach the Guardians' village, depending on how quickly they could move with her. Alone, either one of them could cut that time in half, moving like the wind.

Oliver offered her his sleeping mat and blanket.

"Are you sure?" she asked, wondering how he would do on the ground.

"I insist," he beamed.

"The ground is hard."

"Which is why I insist," he said. He smiled and gave her a nod.

"Thank you," she said.

They hadn't gotten off to the best start, but hopefully, he didn't hate her. Not that she should care, she reminded herself. But she couldn't deny that she did care. Emilia shook off the feeling and settled down on the sleeping mat.

She was exhausted and didn't struggle to sleep, even though it was midday. But sleep brought its own horrors.

In her dream, she was in the courtroom, alone in the seats. The lights were out and only candles illuminated the platform. Her father and mother both stood

Chapter 7

there, hands bound behind their backs and blindfolds across their eyes.

She was weeping, tears trailing down her cheeks, and dripping onto her hands folded in her lap. The liquid was warm and fell like tiny pricks against her fingers. She wanted to cry out to her parents but couldn't open her mouth. She tried to rush to the stage, but her legs were frozen, and her feet were glued to the floor.

The Grand Master appeared from the left; a silver knife clutched in his palm. Fear exploded through her chest, and she struggled against the invisible force holding her perfectly still.

Instead of walking toward her parents, the Grand Master turned and headed for Emilia. He towered over her as he approached, and his face broke into an eerie grin.

"Thank you for bringing your parents' crimes to my attention," he said. "If it weren't for you, they'd have lived." He leaned down and placed a kiss on the top of her head. "I'm so proud of you."

Then he turned and took to the stage. Emilia shook with panic and tried to scream for him to stop. To plead for their lives. To confess that she'd been wrong and made it all up. That she never should have said anything. But she was a statue, trapped inside stone, unable to move, speak, or look away.

The Grand Master walked to her father. He gripped the man's shoulder and held the knife against her father's chest. "For crimes against the Order, you've been found guilty and sentenced to death," he said and killed her father. Unable to move, Emilia watched in horror as the man did the same to her mother.

A hand grabbed her shoulder and pulled her back to the desert. Her scream echoed through the cave. She thrashed against the hand holding her until she became aware that Oliver knelt beside her, eyes worried, holding her firm.

"Emilia, you're okay," he said. "You're here and you're okay."

She stilled under his touch and clamped her hand over her mouth to silence her sobs. It was a dream. No, a nightmare. And not part of reality because the Order didn't execute people that way. Her mind was seeing the worst and none of it was true.

"You're okay," Oliver said again, his voice low and comforting.

Torey knelt beside them, holding a lantern and a steaming cup. She realized for the first time the cave was dark. Night had fallen. Torey set the hot drink down beside her as Oliver released his hold. She immediately felt colder without his touch.

Chapter 7

"When you're ready," Torey said, motioning to the steaming cup. He backed away, leaving the lantern to cast light across her and Oliver.

"I'm sorry," she said.

"Don't be," Oliver said. "I'm sorry for whatever you've faced that haunts your dreams."

Emilia felt she might cry but held her tears. She didn't know what to say.

"I'm going to go help my father pack up. We'll leave soon," Oliver said. Then, he stood and left her with the lantern and the steaming cup. She reached out, fingers still shaking, and took the mug. The liquid smelled like flowers and honey and tasted better than any tea she'd had. It was warm on her tongue and soothed her chest.

She sat still, sipping her drink until her body had calmed and she could stand to roll up her mat. Neither Torey nor Oliver asked her to explain her dream, and soon they were on horses leaving the cave.

But the feeling of shame and dread from her nightmare had wound around her heart like barbed wire. And it traveled with her into the dark desert.

CHAPTER 8

THE FOLLOWING TWO DAYS passed with ease. Emilia, Torey, and Oliver traveled by moonlight and slept in hiding during the hot hours of sunlight. Her inner thighs were sore from riding for so many hours, and she found it hard to sleep for fear of more terrorizing nightmares. But Torey and Oliver cooked delicious meats over fires, offered her more flower tea, and respected her privacy.

They didn't speak much and asked few questions. They rested during the days and traveled during the nights, hunting whatever rabbit or bird presented itself. They saved the salted game from earlier hunting to take home and mostly ate what they could find along the way.

She watched Oliver use his bow and arrows like a seasoned hunter, once taking a rabbit near their camp with a clean shot at fifty paces. He was nearly fifteen and had been hunting since he was six. It showed.

She found herself wishing she could wield a weapon as he did. A few days ago, she'd never thought self-defense skills would be helpful. Everything was different now.

On her third day with them, Emilia awoke before nightfall.

Oliver hovered near and motioned for her to get up.

"What's going on?" she asked.

"We travel through the mountain today," Oliver said. She didn't miss the excitement in his voice and couldn't help but smile.

"*Through* the mountain?" she asked.

"You'll see." He shot her a quick wink and her heart jumped. His excitement was contagious.

She jumped up and helped pack their humble camp. They led the horses out from their cover, and she let Torey help her mount his. They rode across the desert sands for about an hour at a fast clip until they crested a large sand dune, and a towering mountain range came into view.

The sun setting to the west painted a brilliant pink and orange sunset over the peaks. Torey didn't slow his horse as they plunged down the sandy slope toward the mountains. Emilia remembered the range from

Chapter 8

her hand-drawn map and knew they must be close to the Guardians' camp.

Her heart fluttered and excitement prickled her skin. She had no idea what to expect, which made her cling tighter to Torey as they galloped. Soon they came to a small lake, sparkling in the fading sun at the foot of the mountain range. At one end, a roaring waterfall poured down a high cliff. No sign of the camp, but she held her questions as they approached the thundering waterfall.

The mountain face was sharp and steep. The ridges looked like a massive iron fence traveling in either direction for miles. The cliff wasn't climbable, Emilia thought, and she was glad Oliver hadn't said *over* the mountain.

No, he'd said *through*, which was equally confusing. Oliver dismounted as they reached the waterfall. Torey did the same, then helped Emilia down. To see the top, Emilia tilted her chin until she was looking almost entirely skyward. They carefully approached the waterfall, leading the horses, who seemed less afraid than Emilia expected.

"Stay close," Torey said.

Emilia tucked in behind him and held the side of his horse's saddle. The mist from the waterfall brushed her skin. It was freezing in the setting sun, and she held her hand up to protect her eyes as they continued. They walked right up to the base of the waterfall.

She watched as Oliver followed a small stone path that led behind the waterfall and out of sight. Emilia held her breath as she walked with Torey, the water soaking her simple dress. The path took them behind the falling water and into a large cave.

Emilia exhaled and waited for her eyes to adjust to the darkness. The domed ceiling arched above her some fifteen feet and was about that wide across.

"Come," Torey said, offering a blanket to wrap around her wet shoulders.

She accepted, pulling it across herself as Oliver and Torey walked to the left side of the cave. A wide, tall crack exposed a dark and damp tunnel that led farther into the mountain. Torey lit a ball of old cloth that he'd twisted around the top of a thick branch, making a torch to illuminate their way.

Down the tunnel, through twists and turns, they came to another much larger cave, with several more exit tunnels on the opposite side. Delight in this complex cave system replaced Emilia's anxiety. The Guardians lived *in* the mountains. Literally. No wonder they hadn't been found.

After traveling down a few more tunnels that branched off yet another set of caves, daylight began

Chapter 8

to lighten the tunnel walls. After they traveled a few dozen paces further, the sky opened. Emilia felt her breath catch as she stepped into a wide-open area more than four hundred yards deep and wide. Steep, slick, rocky walls encircled the area and towered into the clouds.

Tall wheat and grass fields sat to the east of the open circle. An orchard with fruit trees of all kinds grew beside the fields. A large garden growing a sea of vegetables filled a huge plot of land along the edge of the clearing. Cows, sheep, chickens, horses, and pigs wandered in pens against the western rock walls. Cozy wooden houses with thatched roofs and open windows huddled in the center of everything. Vases of flowers sat on windowsills, and fabric billowed from clotheslines. Trees grew between houses and fruit bushes along small fences. Larger buildings made from stone sat directly in the center, and Emilia imagined their purpose was to serve the community. Maybe they included a school or medical building, a town center, or council hall.

But more surprising than any of those things were the people.

Women were taking down laundry and men were starting cookfires. Workers pulled vendor carts home for the evening and children ran about, trying to avoid trouble. Laughter and warmth filled the air and settled around Emilia like a hug. These were the fabled Guardians. She'd imagined them so differently.

She'd been told they were dangerous rebels threatening the Order, which offered safety and peace. But what she saw before her was just a community of peaceful people.

"Welcome to Mount Zion," Torey said.

Emilia looked at him. Mount Zion.

He handed his horse's reins to Oliver, who'd remounted his horse and now gently nudged the steed toward the animal pens. As he left, he cast a smiling glance at Emilia.

Torey escorted Emilia toward the homes. People caught sight of them as they approached and stopped what they were doing. They started whispering to one another and word spread like fire. From every direction, Guardians took notice of the stranger among them.

Emilia's heart rose into her throat. All the nervousness that had faded with the wonder of it all crept back in. Torey seemed unaffected as he greeted his friends and led Emilia toward the largest stone building. Her eyes searched the faces of the onlookers and saw something she hadn't expected. Fear.

They were afraid of her. None of them spoke, which

Chapter 8

unnerved Emilia even more.

An elderly woman exited the stone building and descended its three wide steps. Her face was wrinkled with time, her skin tinted by the sun. Her dark blue eyes were set in deep wrinkles and her silver hair had been woven into a braid that stretched to her waist. Her flowing dress, the color of chocolate, hung to her feet. A white shawl decorated with fresh flowers and herbs draped her shoulders and was tied neatly at her chest. Leather-braided bands highlighted with colorful stones and dyed ties wrapped both wrists.

The Guardians fell quiet as the woman approached Emilia and Torey. She shared a kind smile with Torey before she pressed her hands to his lips, his forehead, and then his heart; just as he'd done with her father's wooden token.

"It's good to have you back, Brother Torey," she said.

"May my feet always bring me home," he replied.

"And I see you brought someone new," she said, eyes turning to Emilia.

"Desert Mother, this is Emilia. Luca Harker's niece."

Surprise flashed across the old woman's eyes, and whispers rippled through the crowd. The woman raised her hand and brought silence. Her eyes never left Emilia.

"Emilia," she said, her voice warm silk. "My name

The Golden Egg

is Clara. I am the Desert Mother among the people of Zion. Your uncle Luca was among the best of us, and we loved him dearly."

Emilia heard agreed murmurs and caught a few people touching the back of their thumb to their lips, forehead, and heart. She could feel their respect toward the man who shared her last name. She wished she'd known him.

"I can tell from the look in your eyes that you have a story to tell," Clara said. "I would like to hear it."

Emilia wanted to tell her. She was like a grandmother inviting her to sit and share secrets. This made Emilia long for her mother, and she was sure that Clara would help her convince these people to save her.

The Desert Mother raised her hands and addressed the other members of Zion. "Brothers and sisters," she said, "we've been invited into a new opportunity tonight. It's been too long since a stranger joined us, seeking warmth and community. Will you come as love calls you forth? Remember, what you do to the least of these you do to our master. Tonight, we feast in our guest's honor. We join as one, letting our union multiply our joy."

Excited shouts rose into the air. The sky was darkening, and the stars were coming out.

Clara turned back to Emilia with a twinkle in her

Chapter 8

clear eyes. "Will you allow us to celebrate your arrival at our door?"

The playfulness in her tone made Emilia want to giggle. No one had ever thrown a feast in her honor. She was just a girl from Third Ring, but Clara's invitation emboldened her.

Emilia smiled. "Yes," she said softly.

Cheers and laughter went up and people started moving.

"Come with me, child," Clara said. "Let me hear your story while I show you around. Then we will feast." She extended her hand toward Emilia, and Emilia accepted it. The old woman pulled her close and looped her arm through Emilia's; clasping her hand and tapping it gently.

"I always did love a great story," the Desert Mother said.

CHAPTER 9

THE FIRST BUILDING CLARA SHOWED Emilia was the great stone building in Mount Zion's center, which she called the Community Hall—a two-story haven for all in Zion, with a large open space on the bottom floor for events and elders' meetings. The expansive room held a large wooden table and comfortable seating nooks in every cranny, illuminated by glowing lamps. Fluffy blankets and bright pillows filled benches and chairs.

A floor-to-ceiling bookcase stuffed with books of all kinds lined the back wall. Against the east and west walls, stone staircases led to the second floor, a loft big enough for another table that sat eight, with modest lighting and large arched windows to the south.

Just to the east of the Community Hall stood a medical building much smaller than the Community

Hall but well-lit and comfortable. A single stone room contained a half-dozen beds for the sick; and two private side rooms for surgeries or deliveries. It was stocked with supplies either collected on supply runs, which happened twice a year, or made by people in Zion.

On the opposite side of the Community Hall stood a schoolhouse and training facility. All members of Zion were expected to aid in their defense and survival. In addition to basic math, language, and science; children also learned hunting, farming, woodworking, sewing, and cooking. The schoolhouse was divided into six large classrooms with chalkboards, hand-made desks, books, and tools.

The final stone building was small and locked. It housed all their weaponry for hunting and defense, though they hadn't needed to fight any battles in over a hundred years.

More than a hundred and fifty people called Mount Zion home. The dormant volcano had been the Guardian's enclave for over a hundred years. Clara seemed to answer Emilia's questions before she could voice them, all while holding her arm and gently guiding her through their small community. It had been days since such calm filled Emilia's chest. She almost forgot why she was here.

Chapter 9

"So, tell me about you," Clara finally asked as she led Emilia back toward the Community Hall. The calm vanished. Emilia was once again filled with the heartbreak of losing her parents.

She sat beside Clara on the stone steps and told her story. The matriarch listened with intention and compassion. Emilia tried to keep overwhelming emotion from clogging her throat, but everything was raw. Tears dotted her vision, and she prayed they'd stay at bay.

She watched the Guardians prepare the feast. A pig roasted over a sizeable fire inside a permanent stone pit. Flames shot into the sky, licking at the stars and casting a warm, wide glow over the center of Zion. Chairs, tables, blankets, and pillows were brought from homes and set around the roaring fire.

Emilia turned her focus back to the Desert Mother, cutting herself off from the mesmerizing scene. She wanted to talk about rescuing her mother, but a soft pounding drew Emilia's attention back to the fire.

A group of six had gathered on the ground, wooden drums held in their laps. A beautiful, redheaded woman was pounding a soft beat with the heel of her hand while the others nodded in time with the sound. A large man, his long black hair tied at the nape of his neck, joined with a different rhythm that complemented the first beautifully.

"It's time," Clara said and rose from the steps. She offered Emilia her hand and drew the girl toward the music.

All six drummers moved as one as the sound grew in volume and intensity. A small boy, at least a few years younger than Emilia, stepped up beside them and placed a stringed wooden instrument under his chin. He held a long-threaded bow in his other hand and started weaving a fast, delightful sound across the strings of his instrument.

People started clapping and dancing. Some chanted. Children giggled and raced by, fresh flowers twisted around their wrists and hanging around their necks. Some donned crowns made from the same flowers.

A petite girl, pigtail braids of gold cascading over her shoulders and wide brown eyes shining in the firelight, saw the Desert Mother and Emilia coming. She rushed on tiny legs to reach them just outside the gathering, clasping a basket of flowers.

The Desert Mother laughed softly as the child handed her a long necklace of purple and white flowers. Then the girl turned to Emilia, who swallowed as the child looked up at her decisively. The tiny human searched her basket for something specific and pulled out a red-and-yellow flower crown.

Chapter 9

"The flowers chose you," the child said, her voice confident though she was probably only eight.

"They did?" Emilia asked, staring at the flower crown.

"I know flowers, and these chose you," the girl said as if it made perfect sense.

Emilia knew flowers didn't talk, but the light in the child's face was contagious. She took the crown and placed it on her head.

The girl squealed with delight and bounced on her toes. "You look beautiful!" Her tiny hand grabbed Emilia's. "Come on, you have to sit with me."

Emilia glanced at Clara and saw the Desert Mother smile brightly. She could feel the heat from the fire as the girl guided her to a large, thick blanket lined with pillows. The child plopped down and yanked Emilia beside her.

"My name is Isabela, but everyone calls me Izzy," she said.

"My name is E—"

"Emilia. Everyone knows that." Izzy giggled.

Emilia laughed. "Oh, I see."

"You're famous," Izzy whispered.

"I don't think so."

"You are," the girl said matter-of-factly. "Where did you come from?"

Emilia opened her mouth to answer but Izzy continued in a rush.

"Oh, I have so many questions. What is your house like? Do you have other pretty dresses like the one you're wearing? Do you live in the desert? Do you have a pet lizard?" She inhaled sharply, her eyes widening as if she'd just thought of the perfect question. "Have you ever seen a dragon?"

The question chilled Emilia's skin, and her mouth fell open. The girl didn't look scared at all when she used *that* word. She didn't lower her voice or check to ensure no one was listening. She said it as if it was commonplace, not forbidden. *Dragon*. Emilia went numb.

"You don't have to answer her questions," a familiar voice said from behind.

Emilia turned to see Oliver step onto the blanket where they sat, another teen boy beside him. The newcomer's hair was amber-red, and hundreds of matching freckles dotted his face. He was taller than Oliver and shaped like a bean pole, all arms and legs.

"She wants to answer my questions," Izzy fired back. "We're new friends."

Oliver chuckled and sat between Izzy and Emilia. The new boy settled on the other side of Izzy. "Maybe give her a night to settle in," Oliver said with a playful

Chapter 9

punch to the child's shoulder and a teasing glance toward Emilia.

Izzy considered Oliver's plea and then frowned. "Fine," Izzy said and shot her eyes to Emilia. "Promise you'll eat breakfast with me tomorrow?"

"Sure," Emilia answered softly.

Izzy clapped her hands together in delight.

"Isabela," a voice called across the fire.

"That's my mom. I gotta go," Izzy said and bounced to her feet. She skipped off the blanket toward the flames, humming to the music as she went. Emilia couldn't help but smile after her, even as the word *dragon* buzzed at the back of her brain. Her eyes followed the girl until she disappeared behind the roaring fire.

"Don't mind her, she's just curious," Oliver said. "I'm not sure she's ever seen a stranger."

The music continued to play as two large men carried the roasted pig to be carved. Singing rose into the air as fruit and vegetables were diced and passed for consumption. Emilia's eyes followed the drifting smoke and caught the dark sky. Bright and clear, filled with millions of stars. Her father would have loved it. She longed for him, for her mother. What would they think of Zion?

"How did the desert elders find this place?" Emilia

asked, her voice filled with wonder.

"The spirit of the true prophet, Jack Solomon, led the elders here. He lived during the time of dragons. His and his son's teaching of love over fear guides our people while we wait. It brought us here, and the elders named the mountain Zion."

Emilia knew the name Jack Solomon. She'd read about him briefly in her histories. He had come from space after the great religious wars and made a way for humanity to return to a dragon-infested planet.

"Led the elders here for what?" she asked.

Oliver hesitated. "To wait," he said.

"Wait for what?"

Oliver looked at her as if trying to decide whether to reveal some great secret. Instead of answering, he nodded toward the redhead. "This is Brodie by the way," he said.

"Hiya," Brodie said with a wave of his fingers. "So, you're from Capital City. Do you really leave the bodies of criminals hanging from gallows in the streets to remind people of what happens when they break the law?"

Emilia felt like she'd been punched.

"Seriously?" Oliver rebuked his friend.

"What?" the boy said, his tone on the verge of laughter, his hands raised in feigned innocence. "It's a thing I heard."

Chapter 9

Anger coiled in Emilia's chest. "Do you really eat the dead you find in the desert?" she asked.

Both boys, wide-eyed, looked at her.

"It's a thing I heard," Emilia shot back.

A beat passed, and then both boys started to laugh. Emilia smiled. It was clear that what she'd been taught about the Guardians was false.

Her father's words whispered through her mind: *There is more to this world than you know.* Was this what he'd meant? She hadn't spent much time thinking about it, but now curiosity mixed with her sadness, and Emilia wished she could have asked him. Why, of all things, he had chosen to say that as his last words?

A loud clang echoed through the village, and Brodie jumped to his feet. "Finally, I'm starving."

"The feast is ready," Oliver explained while he stood and offered Emilia his hand. She took it and he pulled her up.

"We don't eat people," Brodie said, walking backward. "However, we do eat well."

"And, if you're Brodie, every five minutes," Oliver teased.

"Look at all this muscle I have to feed," Brodie returned, flexing his skinny arms.

Emilia chuckled as Oliver rolled his eyes and followed the boy toward the feast. Her stomach growled loudly, and a splash of embarrassment scorched her face.

Brodie's smile widened. "See, Emilia knows what it's like to need to eat. Don't shame us." He threw Emilia a wink, and she decided that she liked Brodie very much regardless of what he thought about Capital City.

Oliver shook his head, but his smile was bright. Emilia liked him too. In fact, she hadn't met a person in Mount Zion she didn't like. Which brought confusion considering all the nasty things she'd been taught about them. Again, her father's words whispered to her.

There is more to this world than you know.

She wondered what else about the world would prove to be more than it appeared.

✦✦✦

Brodie was right. The people of Zion feasted well. Emilia's stomach was stuffed with warm, delicious food; unlike anything she'd tasted before. Of course, in Capital City, eating for survival was necessary. But eating for pleasure was discouraged, at least in the lower ring where she grew up; probably so the citizens wouldn't complain about their bland food, Emilia thought in retrospect. But here, everyone ate like they were in heaven.

Chapter 9

She ate the perfectly seasoned meats and vegetables until she couldn't possibly take another bite.

Then, without warning, Izzy swept across the crowd and grabbed Emilia to join their dance circle. For a moment, Emilia feared she would throw up, but the music captured her feet and heart. She twirled with Izzy hand-in-hand, smiling so wide her cheeks hurt. The stars danced and laughter filled Mount Zion.

The night finally settled as the music faded and what food remained was carried away for another meal. Torey and Oliver led Emilia away from the doused fire and to a small canvas tent erected for her beside the Community Hall.

"Clara assumed you'd like a bit of privacy," Torey said. "The weather should be fair, and I stuffed it full of furs and blankets. You're protected from the rising sun's glare here, so hopefully you can get some rest."

Emilia felt overcome by his kindness. "Thank you."

He gave her a nod and placed a soft hand on her shoulder. "If you need anything, we're just there." He pointed to a small wooden square home with a lit window about a hundred paces away. "Don't hesitate to come knock. Or, if you're more comfortable, Clara lives on the corner there. Her door is open as well."

Emilia nodded, the heaviness of the last days suddenly crashing over her. Exhaustion beckoned her to sleep, and she was glad to have her own space. Torey gave her shoulder a squeeze and then left. Oliver stayed behind and waited till his father was nearly out of earshot.

"I never did say I was sorry," Oliver said.

"For what?"

"For what happened to your father."

Emilia wondered if her heart would ever stop aching at the thought of him.

"I know what it's like to lose a parent," Oliver said. "My mother passed two years ago. She was always sick, and her body couldn't handle it anymore."

He rubbed the back of his neck and seemed uncomfortable. Emilia understood that better than she wanted to.

"I'm telling you because I want you to know you're not alone," Oliver said. "You're safe here."

She didn't know what to say. Thank you sounded lame, but other words failed her. Oliver gave her a final glance and then turned to follow his father. Emilia watched for a long moment before pushing aside the flap of her tent.

Torey hadn't lied. The small space was filled with comfort. She removed her shoes and found a clean tunic left for her. It was a bit big but clean and warm. She lay on the thick sleeping mat and pulled blankets

Chapter 9

up to her chin. She closed her eyes and immediately saw the faces of her parents.

The joy of the feasting had swallowed her for a time and numbed her pain. But in the quiet dark, sorrow flowed like a roaring river threatening to drag her beneath the surface. Silent tears streamed down her cheeks, and she opened her eyes.

She could do nothing for her father, but tomorrow she would convince Clara to help her save her mother. She couldn't—wouldn't—stop until she was with her mother again.

Mother was all Emilia had in this world, and without her this pain would drown her.

CHAPTER 10

VICTORIA STOOD ON THE DARK rocky ground that surrounded the Keep. Heavy storm clouds blocked the sun's rays. She'd arrived at the Keep an hour ago, after a two-day ride north from Capital City. The Keep was a sanctuary for the Overseers, who worshiped the sanctity of the human spirit and the law created by the Order. At least, that's what the Grand Master and the members of the Order council believed.

After Sylas had destroyed the last dragon and started the Order a hundred and fifty years ago, he had established the Overseers to ensure every Grand Master and Order council followed the law. Following the law ensured peace and control.

Victoria grew up with the same history as everyone else. Humanity had tried to destroy itself twice, once with technology, starting an epic war that sent humans into space to survive the global destruction. The melting of the ice caps caused by those wars allowed ancient dragon eggs to hatch and flood the earth with dragons—the red, black, and purple ones born of fear, and the silver ones born of love, it was said. The stench of the dragons of fear had poisoned the air and made it impossible for humans to return from space once their oxygen and food ran out.

But a lone boy, Jack Solomon, had overcome the odds and returned to defeat the red dragons with the help of the silver dragons.

Still, many humans joined the Reds and sought to kill the Silvers and their protectors. For the next one hundred years, humans and dragons waged a bloody war.

Peace came only when the warlord Sylas declared war on *all* dragons and created the Order.

With its code of strictly enforced laws, including the law that banned any mention of dragons, the Order ensured humanity never destroyed itself again. Everyone outside that law—the heretics of the desert, these Guardians—threatened that safety with their rebellion.

Only conformity assured safety. Anything that broke the codes of conformity established individuality. Individuality led to rebellion, and rebellion always led to war.

Chapter 10

Victoria agreed in principle, but, as an Overseer, she knew more than most. What the Order did *not* know—what the Overseers were protecting and advancing—was much more significant than the law. It's why the Keep existed. It was built by Sylas's eldest son, Malcolm, the first Overseer.

Malcolm disagreed that all dragons should be destroyed and instead believed in the power of the dark dragons as allies. So, he preserved a single black dragon egg inside the Keep and waited for it to hatch. It birthed the beautiful dragon queen now living in the massive caves beneath the Keep. For generations, the Overseers had protected the dragon by hiding her and her red eggs from the world.

Some would say Malcolm's heart was wicked, but Victoria knew this judgment came from small-minded people. He'd been a visionary. One day all would understand Malcom's wisdom. She never thought that day would happen in her lifetime, but now she knew it would.

That was the gift Silvia and Emilia would give her—a gift they didn't yet understand. If they were right, if the Guardians really did have a golden egg in their possession, it could only mean that the time for ultimate confrontation had finally arrived. She would crush the Guardians and their golden egg, along with their pitiful belief that a gold dragon would rise and return the world to peace through love, rather than peace enforced by law.

Victoria inhaled, approached a small stone altar outside the Keep, and set the large, red dragon egg upon the fire. She knew what to expect, but her heart quickened as she took a few steps back and waited.

She performed this ritual once a month, during the New Moon Ceremony, offering the blood of an unhatched dragon to satisfy the demands of fear. Although the Order had forbidden all dragon lore and burned all texts mentioning them, Malcolm had saved a few books. Victoria studied them repeatedly, as had every Overseer before her.

She watched a ray of sun cut through the clouds and alight on the red egg. Time ticked by and her heart slowed. She'd been waiting longer than usual, she thought. Maybe . . .

The red egg began to shake. The egg's surface cracked. Black smoke edged from the crack and rose into the air as the creature inside burned to death.

Victoria refused to look away. The dragon that burned deserved this honor as it died in the same way hundreds had been killed. The egg stilled and after a few moments the smoke dwindled to a wisp. The crack at the top crept along the face of the egg and the shell

Chapter 10

split in half, falling apart into two sections. Nothing inside but ash. It was always just ash. One day soon, red dragons would be hatched, but for now, the ash served to remind the Overseers that their life was nothing without the power of the dragons.

Victoria swallowed her momentary grief and turned on her heels. The Keep loomed ahead as a bright crack of lightning laced the dark clouds behind it. As Victoria headed for the large arched entrance, the air smelled like rain. The Keep stood on a large plateau with a single narrow road that ran down the mountain to the valley. It was constructed of massive cut stones and bricks, still as strong as the day of its construction, towering into the clouds like an old, vast cathedral. There were no windows. It was a prison that kept the dragon in, and unwelcome humans out.

Victoria walked up the wide, stone steps and through the large wooden doors. Two solemn men in long gray cloaks closed the doors behind her and sealed them with iron bars. Hand-selected by the Overseer, the Keepers, one hundred of them, lived their entire lives in the Keep. The air in and around the Keep was deadly, survivable only by those who regularly drank dragon's milk.

Victoria's steps echoed across the stone floor as the rain began to fall outside. Inside, large stone archways rose toward high chandeliers with blazing candles that lit the room and filled it with shadows. A massive sanctuary lined with wooden pews took up the majority of the first floor. Two thick stone pillars marked the sanctuary's entrance, each draped in a large silver banner with an embroidered image of an oak tree, which represented the Order. The symbol was a sign of life—strong yet bending its branches to the law.

The two floors above the main sanctuary contained humble rooms that housed the Keepers. The marble stage at the back of the main sanctuary held six iron candelabras, their arms like antlers, housing lit candles that dripped wax onto the floor. Another enormous Order banner hung on the wall behind the stage. This was mere signaling to visitors such as the Grand Master, who must be led to believe the Keep existed as an arm of the Order.

The Grand Master, Martin, had visited twice since Victoria had become Overseer, and both times he agreed the Keep was a holy place for the Overseers' reflection and solitude. Martin had asked once why there were no windows, and Victoria told him it was to keep the world out and maintain purity. This was the truth, just not in the way the Grand Master suspected.

Victoria cut toward an unassuming door in the corner of the sanctuary. A short bald man draped in

Chapter 10

gray stood beside it. This was Lee Towers, the High Keeper and head authority of the Keep whenever Victoria was away. The man was in his late seventies and had served two Overseers.

As Victoria approached, Lee pulled an iron key from his waistband.

"All is as it was?" he asked, knowing the answer.

Victoria nodded. "For now."

Lee unlocked the door and let Victoria step through first before following. They were met by a long stone hallway, wall-mounted candle sconces every few yards lighting their path. Lee pulled the door shut and locked it with a bolt. He stepped around Victoria and led her down the narrow path that led into the underground levels.

They said nothing as they walked the long tunnel and approached another locked door, this one iron. Lee pulled another key from its place at his waist and twisted the bolt free with a click that echoed through the hall.

A lengthy, narrow staircase wound down into the massive underground cave. Lee grabbed a lantern on the first step and lit the candle inside. The flame flickered as they began their descent. Victoria couldn't see the bottom of the staircase, and the air around her was dank. Two distinct smells filled her nostrils: the smoke of burning coals and the sweet scent of dragon's milk.

As Lee led them down the steps he reached behind the breast of his cloak and retrieved a small vial. The vessel was filled with a creamy substance. Her pulse quickened at the sight of fluid, and she craved it to her bones. She popped the small cork that sealed the vial and drained its contents. Dragon's milk mixed with honey and vinegar. The moment the liquid touched her tongue, Victoria felt it. Felt *her*.

Come, the voice cooed for only Victoria to hear.

A hundred years before the Order, people who drank dragons' milk grew dragon scales. It clouded their eyes and made them entirely subservient to fear. They required the milk to survive the poison the dark dragons released into the atmosphere.

The Overseers, including Malcolm and Victoria, never grew scales. Some said the honey and vinegar, added by alchemists who served the dragons, prevented this. Victoria didn't know, but she was grateful. Scales would be hard to explain to the Grand Master.

The dragon's milk seeped into her stomach, and she was sure she could feel the mother's heartbeat. The elixir connected Victoria to the milk's provider and allowed them to communicate. The effects lasted only a few days, though Victoria longed for the connection at all times.

Chapter 10

Come, the voice whispered again.

Victoria stepped off the final stair and followed Lee deeper into the chamber. The ceiling disappeared into darkness and the walls were covered in deep shadows. To the right, three Keepers tended a fire, smoke ascending toward the cave's highest point. There was enough light to see their feet as they rounded a corner into the massive den.

The ground shook as the beast there moved, still shrouded in darkness. Victoria bowed in respect as always and heard the purr of acceptance. Glancing up, Victoria saw two golden eyes glowing in the dark. The ground rumbled again as the mother stepped closer.

Victoria settled to one knee. "My queen," she said.

The dragon's scales started to glow fifty paces away. Bright purple lit the darkness as the glow spread from one scale to the next, starting at the mother's tail and finishing with the scales between her golden eyes.

Awe filled Victoria's chest. No matter how often she witnessed the creature, the beauty took her aback. The dragon queen towered fifty feet tall and three times as long from head to tail. The end of her tail housed three sharp spikes that could easily cut a man in half. She had legs as thick as oak trunks, and her tucked wings, leathery and smooth, lay on either side of her torso. Black talons, four on each foot, scraped the stone with each movement. Her twelve-foot snout stretched long from her neck, concealing rows of razor-sharp teeth.

Behind her along the sides of the cave, small alcoves held her red dragon eggs, none of which could hatch.

Not yet.

Rise, my child, the dragon said. Only Victoria could hear, but Lee stood close by as always. Victoria rose.

I felt the death of my offspring, the dragon spoke. *I grow tired of this heartbreak.*

"It's what we require to remind ourselves that we have power and yet are nothing without you."

To this, the mother dragon said nothing.

"But I believe change is coming," Victoria continued. "Something has happened."

Say it.

"I have new evidence that the desert heretics have the golden egg."

The dragon hissed, her sound rattling the loose stone around the cave.

Explain.

"I discovered a letter that confirms the Guardians have seen the egg. Considering their belief in the prophecy, it's not farfetched to believe they would stay close to it."

So, you do not know where they are.

Victoria swallowed. "No, but I intercepted a mother

Chapter 10

and daughter fleeing the city for the Guardian camp. The mother was caught, but the daughter got away. I sent out five hundred soldiers in every direction to track the girl, in the hopes she'll lead us to the Guardian camp."

For one hundred and fifty years, Overseers have sought the golden egg created by the Silvers. The dragon's eyes flashed with hatred. *None have been able to find it and free me. As long as that golden egg lives, I am trapped here. My offspring, born of the fear that rules humanity, will never hatch.*

"I know, my queen," Victoria said. "I will not be like those that failed you. The letter was hand-delivered to its recipient, so it couldn't have traveled far. I have a feeling the Guardians are closer than we ever thought. I will find them. I swear it to you."

The anger rolling off the mother dragon eased. *The golden egg must be destroyed before it hatches.*

"It's sat dormant for over a century, my queen. Only a worthy soul chosen by the Silvers can awaken it. That soul won't find the egg before I do. I dare say there is no such soul alive today."

If that egg hatches and the dragon within comes into its fullness, I dare say that all of humanity will suffer in ways never before seen.

"That won't happen."

The dragon surveyed Victoria for a long moment, then released a hot breath through her nostrils. It washed over Victoria, the power rippling over her skin and forcing her to one knee. Moist heat sank through her clothes and settled across her flesh. It was pain and pleasure, but primarily, a fog of fear that surrounded Victoria's heart.

Do not make a promise to me you cannot keep, child.

Victoria opened her mouth to speak, and the heat rushed into her throat, choking her words. Her shoulders shook with terror and her brain seized.

Is that clear?

"Yes," Victoria managed, and the release of fear was immediate.

Victoria gasped, forcing air into her lungs as the heat turned to icy cold. She was glad the terror was gone but longed for the warmth. To fear something and desire it so deeply twisted Victoria's gut.

Victoria pushed herself back to her feet, her limbs still shaking, and raised her eyes to the dragon. The scales' purple glow was beginning to fade, an indicator that the mother dragon was nearly finished with her.

Do not fail me.

Victoria's heart thumped. *Daughter.* The dragon mother only called her favorites by such an affirmation. And she'd never bestowed it on Victoria. Profound

Chapter 10

determination filled her bones, and with it came the sweet comfort that only came from the dragon's milk. One second the dragon mother was raining down fear; the next moment she was giving adoration.

And Victoria accepted both.

In all things be vigilant, child. In all things be true.

"Yes, my queen," Victoria said, as the ground shook with the dragon's retreating steps. The soft purple hue faded to black, and the beast disappeared into the darkness. But Victoria could still feel the mother under her skin. And she could feel the queen as she followed Lee back up the winding stone steps; down the long dark hallway; and into the sanctuary, where she found a place to sit among the empty pews.

The dragon queen was with her. Victoria let her presence flow under her skin as she stared at the silver Order banner with its intricately embroidered oak tree.

She would play her part as Overseer and find the golden egg. Then she would serve her true queen and release the dragons into the skies.

CHAPTER 11

EMILIA OPENED HER EYES slowly as the soft sounds of morning filtered through the sides of her tent. She stretched her arms and sat up, the heaviness of sleep falling off her shoulders. She'd slept like a rock for the first time in days. Her dreams were free of nightmares and her body felt rested.

She stood and dressed in another set of fresh clothes left the night before. The cotton pants were soft, fitting her waist and then billowing slightly for mobility before cinching at her ankles. They were light blue, the same color as the matching long-sleeved tunic. The garment was long, ending just past her hips. A thin fabric belt looped around her waistline, and Emilia tied it into a bow at her middle. The outfit fit well. Thick cream socks and brown ankle boots completed the ensemble. She brushed her tangled, dark hair and secured it in a long ponytail at the nape of her neck.

Emilia ran her fingers over the front of her tunic and tried to imagine how she looked. Clean. Comfortable. Rested. Better than she had in days. It was a good place to start, and she was grateful to whomever had given her these clothes.

She pushed from her tent into the crisp morning air. The people of Zion were awake and moving. Children scurried toward the schoolhouse. Women and men were already working in the gardens and with the livestock. People walked to and fro with gathered food, tools, and other supplies.

"Good morning."

Emilia jumped and turned at the voice coming from the Community Hall steps. Oliver stood, Brodie beside him.

"Hi," Emilia said.

"We've been assigned to you today," Brodie said.

"Assigned," Emilia replied. She didn't need a babysitter. Then again, maybe here in a strange place she did.

"He just means we were asked to show you the ropes," Oliver explained. "Make sure you don't feel lost."

"That's basically what I said," Brodie said with a shrug.

Emilia shook her head but smiled. "Okay. Well, then maybe some breakfast first?"

Chapter 11

Brodie leaped down from the second step and dramatically slapped a hand over his chest. "A girl after my own heart."

"You already had breakfast," Oliver said.

"Second breakfast is a thing, my brother," Brodie replied.

"I promised Izzy I'd eat with her," Emilia said.

"Breakfast and integration," Oliver teased. "You have quite the morning planned."

Emilia chuckled. The sun was warm, and the sky was bright blue, filled with fluffy clouds. Birds swept through the air and for a moment Emilia didn't feel the sting of grief that had constantly consumed her.

"They're back!" someone shouted across the valley to Emilia's right. She turned to see a young woman, maybe in her twenties, pointing toward the north rock wall and waving. Emilia followed the woman's gaze and saw six horses with riders crossing toward the center of the compound. They rode in a triangle formation led by a broad man with graying hair and a stern expression. He looked every bit the warrior.

Emilia crossed her arms over her chest, feeling suddenly cautious.

"That's Bastien Ward, Zion's Protector and one of the desert elders. Second only to our Desert Mother," Oliver explained. His name rang with familiarity.

Oliver had mentioned him when they found her in the desert.

"The two that flank him are Russo and Marcs, best hunters in Zion," Oliver continued. "Helen and Saul are the other two riders. Helen can shoot anything with an arrow."

"From the back of a horse at a full gallop," Brodie added. "And Saul's more bloodhound than man. Man's a tracking legend."

"They've been gone for nearly three weeks collecting supplies and—"

"Spying," Brodie said, cutting Oliver off.

"Spying?" Emilia asked.

"Gathering intel on the state of the Order," Oliver said.

"Always best to know what your enemy is doing," Brodie said.

Fear bloomed in Emilia. The Order thought desert heretics were the enemy, but hearing it put this way made *her* feel like the enemy.

The man Oliver had identified as Bastien pulled his horse to a stop in the center of Zion and dismounted. His team followed. He handed his reins to Russo, and the man led the horses toward the fields where the other animals grazed. Saul took the horses that belonged to Helen and Marcs, leaving them standing with Bastien.

Chapter 11

Helen was a petite woman in her forties. Her short black hair fell in a slant across her face and hid one of her brown eyes. Her lips were thin, her chin sharp, and an aged scar ran through her left eyebrow. Marcs stood a foot taller than Helen but was short compared to Bastien. He looked older than the woman, with shaved white hair. His skin was dark brown, his eyes deep blue, and his full lips smiled as a beautiful woman embraced him. Clearly his wife.

"Father!" The young woman who'd announced their arrival bounced across the grass and threw her arms around Bastien's neck. He smiled, softening as he returned her embrace. "Welcome home," the daughter said.

Bastien began to speak as his eyes swept across those gathered, but when he reached Emilia he froze for a moment and shut his mouth. The warmth his daughter brought to his eyes vanished, and the cold edge returned. Emilia's heart surged and she dropped her eyes to the dirt.

Before Bastien could move or speak, another strode to greet the party from behind Emilia.

"Bastien," Clara said. "Welcome back. Helen and Marcs, what a joy this day brings."

"Thank you, Desert Mother," Helen said, clutching Clara's hand. "The days away have been long."

The Golden Egg

Clara extended her other hand toward Marcs, who accepted it. "Coming home is always a joy."

Clara released their hands and turned to Bastien. "I'm excited to hear of your journey, my brother."

Emilia watched as Bastien's eyes found her again. He stepped around the Desert Mother. "Who let this outsider into our camp?"

The Guardians fell quiet. Only the breeze in the branches and the livestock moving through the fields made any sound for a long moment.

"I did," Torey said, stepping from behind another couple. "Oliver and I found her in the desert."

"And you thought it wise to bring her here?" Bastien asked.

"She is but a child," Clara said.

"I know who she is," Bastien said. The words sent a chill through Emilia, and she tried to remove her gaze from the man but couldn't. "Capital City has hundreds of Order Guards searching for her as we speak."

Hushed murmurs spread through the crowd. *Hundreds*, Emilia thought. She was that much of a threat to the city? If the Grand Master had sent hundreds of Order Guards to find her, what had become of her mother?

"You're certain?" Clara asked.

Bastien nodded. "Saul heard whispers of a girl who

Chapter 11

fled the city and evaded capture. They want her found at all costs. We narrowly avoided detection ourselves."

"But you did," Clara said. "And they'll not find her here."

Bastien moved his gaze to the Desert Mother. "How can you be sure? Playing with fate is dangerous, Clara."

They stared at each other briefly before the Desert Mother cleared her throat and turned to the watchful eyes. "Do not be afraid, Zion," she said. "The desert elders will meet immediately and determine the best course of action. Please return to your chores."

Another beat of silence passed before the people heeded the Desert Mother's words and returned to their work. Emilia watched as Bastien and Clara shared whispered words that Emilia couldn't hear before Clara turned to Helen.

"Gather the elders," the Desert Mother said.

Helen gave a single nod and left. Clara walked toward Emilia, softening her expression and offering a hand. "Come," she said. "It's time for you to meet the rest of the elders."

CHAPTER 12

EMILIA SAT IN ONE OF THE ROOMS in the second story of the Community Hall. The bottom level had been cleared and the front doors shut. Before her was a long birchwood table surrounded by the seven elders, eyes fixed on her. Four she knew, three she did not.

The Desert Mother, Clara, and the protector, Bastien, occupied the center seats. Beside Bastien sat Helen, the one who could supposedly shoot anything with an arrow. Beside Clara sat Torey, a reassuring smile on his face. Emilia was so happy to discover the man who had rescued her from the desert was here.

Beside Helen sat a younger man, Amos, with a full black beard and bald head. The man was built like a truck, broad enough to need two chairs, though he balanced on one, and beside him sat his wife, Maria.

The Golden Egg

She was small in comparison, but then Emilia imagined most people were small compared to Amos. Emilia knew without needing to be told that this woman with tight blond curls and bright brown eyes was Izzy's mother. The child was a mini version of Maria.

Finally, a man named Arthur occupied the last seat beside Torey. He sported a white beard, not as thick and long as Amos's, matching the long white hair that graced the tops of his shoulders. His eyes were hazel and held her gaze with fascination.

They had been talking back and forth for a few minutes, Emilia saying nothing. She wasn't really listening, too busy imagining they would throw her back into the desert, where she would either die on her own or be found and executed by the Order Guard. The wind swept in through the open arched window and swept a thin strand of hair across her cheek. She returned her focus to the present.

"She must be important for an army of guards to be looking for her," Helen said.

"She's the daughter of a seamstress," Clara said in a defensive tone.

"Then why the pursuit?" Bastien asked.

"Perhaps this has something to do with Luca?" Amos asked.

"It's been fifty years since such a large force was sent

Chapter 12

into the desert. Why now?" Maria questioned.

"This is dangerous, Clara," Bastien said.

"So you have said," Clara responded.

Torey cleared his throat. "Maybe we could talk to her instead of about her. She is standing before us."

The room fell silent, and all eyes turned to Emilia. She swallowed and clenched her hands in her lap so they wouldn't see them trembling.

"Why are these warriors after you, my dear?" Torey asked.

"I broke the law," Emilia answered. "I fled without permission. Punishment will be the price for my actions."

Sadness shone in Clara's eyes. "And you believe you deserve this punishment?"

Emilia shrugged. "The law keeps us safe. It ensures peace."

"It instills fear," Clara said.

"Better to be afraid than to be dead," Emilia said without thinking. Many in Capital City used this phrase.

Silence filled the space. The Desert Mother seemed to be considering her words carefully. "Fear is a living death, my child."

Emilia didn't understand what that meant, but it stirred something she couldn't identify in her heart.

"You speak like a true believer in the Order," Bastien said.

"I was," Emilia said, then realized her slip-up. "I mean, I am." But that wasn't a hundred percent true. "I mean..." She stumbled, confused by her own feelings. Confusion was life-threatening. Her father had been confused, and now he was dead. The Order allowed no second-guessing of its laws.

"You seem lost," Torey spoke softly.

Emilia wanted to snap at him. Of course she was lost! Her whole life had fallen apart.

"I was certain," she said. "But then one of your Guardians confused my father. He changed and now..." Angry tears filled her eyes. "You destroyed my life." Emilia knew it wasn't fair, but she couldn't stop herself from saying it.

"The Order took your father from you," Bastien said, keeping his voice soft. "We did not."

His words reminded Emilia of something similar her mother had said: *You're not to blame for this. This isn't your doing. It's theirs.* The law was clear, and her father had broken it, but who had her father harmed? What trouble had he caused?

The Order told her the law kept its people safe from those who didn't follow it. But who had been kept safe from her father's offense? Where was the proof of what

Chapter 12

they had always told her? And what about her mother, who had done nothing? It all started to jumble in her mind.

"Did the Order send you?" Bastien asked abruptly, glaring at her.

"Bastien," Clara said in voice that suggested he calm his tone.

But Bastien wasn't interested in calm "We don't know her intentions! She's not one of us, and we only trust our own."

Torey held up the token that had come to her father. "She carried this token and one of Luca's maps," he said. "And she shares our blood. Luca was her uncle."

"Blood has betrayed us before," Bastien countered.

"You believe they sent a child spy to collect secrets?" Maria asked.

"That's a bit of a reach, Bastien," Amos said. "Why send Order Guards after a spy they sent?"

Emilia held to the word *secrets*. It drew her back to last night. What had Oliver said? The spirit of the true prophet, Jack Solomon, led the elders here to wait. But wait for what? Oliver wasn't willing to say. A question popped into her brain. If she could discover this secret, could she trade that information to the Order for her mother?

The thought appeared so quickly she didn't have

time to rebuke it. It was a terrible thing to consider. These people had been nothing but kind to her, at least until Bastien arrived. There were innocent children here, and Emilia knew better than anyone what the Order did to its enemies. She couldn't imagine betraying these people, but she would do anything to save her mother.

"She has nowhere else to go," Torey said. "We can't in good conscience send her out into the desert."

"No," Bastien said. "She could lead the Order Guards back to our door."

"Always certain of trouble," Clara said to Bastien.

"You were called to nurture our people as we continue our mission," Bastien said. "And I was called to protect our people while we wait."

There it was again. Wait for what? Emilia racked her memories for anything she had overheard her father say in those last weeks that might give her a clue. He had talked about the Guardians, their sacred call, and the belief that the world was more than it appeared to be. He had mentioned dragons, but in what context she'd never known.

Emilia worked up her courage and spoke. "What's your mission?"

The room turned to her in silence.

Clara was the first to speak. "What do you know of us here?"

Chapter 12

"Very little. The Order says you're heretics who want to poison our minds and draw us into danger. They say you want to be gods who rebel rather than follow the safety of the law. You want chaos and you threaten peace."

Arthur chuckled at the end of the table. It was the first time he'd made any sound. "The same nonsense they've been spewing for a hundred years," he said.

"If it isn't true, then who are you?" Emilia asked. "Why live outside the Order? This choice puts you at great risk."

Clara shifted and before she could speak Bastien lay a hand on her arm as if to say, *Be careful what you tell her*. He and Clara exchanged a glance before she spoke.

"We are descendants of mystics once known as the Seers. We follow the way of love, which was shown to the world through the true prophet, Jack Solomon, and his eldest son, Noah. They believed in the teachings of Yeshua, in the way of love, a way brought about during the Great Awakening over two hundred years ago."

"Oliver told me the spirit of Jack Solomon led you here," Emilia said.

Clara smiled. "Not in a physical sense, but Jack Solomon followed the love of Yeshua, which also guides us, as it guided those who came before us." She indicated the council. "Our ancestors taught us the secret way of love, and we will do the same for our descendants."

"I've never heard of the Great Awakening," Emilia said.

"The Order keeps much from its people," Torey said. "You've heard of the great religious wars that sent humans into space and released dragons on the Earth?"

Emilia nodded. "Jack Solomon made a way for humanity to return. That is what I know of him."

Torey nodded. "Jack chose love over fear and invited others to follow. Before that, our histories show that people were subjected to the dragons of fear that poisoned the air. After Jack revealed a path of salvation through the teachings of Yeshua, many joined the community of Seers. The event became known as the Great Awakening, and for a time there was true peace."

"Only for a time?" Emilia asked.

"Fear found its way back into the heart of humanity. Red dragons began to flood the skies, and the truth of the Great Awakening started to fade," Bastien said. "The Seers did what they could, alongside the Silvers, the kind and wise dragons that have always been a friend to humanity."

Emilia felt her eyes widen and shook her head. "Good dragons?" she whispered, then felt guilty for speaking the forbidden term. Emilia inhaled and

Chapter 12

spoke what she believed. "All dragons have always been enemies to humans."

"That's a lie fabricated by Sylas and perpetrated by the Order, which he established," Bastien said. "Only the Red dragons were. Sylas ignored the call to love and created a system of law ruled by fear. Silvers joined the Seers to end the madness."

Clara finished for him. "Sylas hunted and killed all Silvers and almost all Seers—only a handful managed to escape."

Emilia's mind tried to digest all they were saying, but it went against so much that she'd been taught.

"The Seers that survived hid in the desert while Sylas built his kingdom," Bastien said, disdain in his tone. Clara and Bastien shared a knowing look.

"What happened next?" Emilia asked, sensing the story wasn't finished.

She was met with silence.

"Tell the girl the truth," Arthur said. He seemed to be a man of few words, but when he spoke, people listened. "Stop looking at her with your eyes and look at her with your heart. She is Luca's niece, which means the blood of the true prophet runs through her veins."

"Arthur!" Bastien warned.

"What?" Emilia exclaimed at the same time.

"Enough of this, Bastien," Arthur scolded. "Your

fear blinds you."

Arthur turned to Emilia and leaned forward on the table. "You're a Harker, yes?"

"Yes," Emilia answered.

"The same blood that flowed in Luca's veins flows in you, my girl. He and his family were descendants of the true prophet, Jack Solomon. You are a descendant of the Seers!" He pounded his fist on the table and Emilia jumped. "You may be blinded to the truth, but I can see you."

The world seemed to narrow so that only the bright eyes of Arthur remained.

"You sense in your bones there is more to this world than you know." He continued, "You just have to open your heart to it."

Those were her father's exact words. Tears blurred her vision as she turned from the old man and the rest of the room came back into view. She felt the stirring. She wanted to know what they were keeping from her. She needed to know.

Clara shared another look with Bastien, who gave her a slight nod of acceptance.

"After Sylas destroyed the last dragon, the remaining Seers hid in the desert for nearly fifty years, until a prophecy was given in a dream," Clara said. "The prophecy changed the course of our people. It stated

Chapter 12

that a way had been made for us to liberate the world from the tyranny of the Order. We were to seek out a new kind of dragon. A Gold, unhatched in a golden egg. The Gold dragon and its rider will bring freedom from the law that persecutes us."

Emilia didn't know what to do with this claim. She spoke before considering her words.

"A... A dragon exists?"

"Yes," Torey said. "We protect it here, within Mount Zion. The spirit led our ancestors here because the egg is here."

Emilia's breathing slowed, heavy with fear. A forbidden dragon egg was in this mountain?

"We wait until the rider appears and the egg hatches for them," Clara said.

Emilia was hardly listening, Her mind was still hung on the word *dragon*. "You've... You've seen this egg?"

Clara nodded and Emilia sat back, numb. Arthur stood and rounded the table, but Emilia barely noticed.

"But to even think about dragons is forbidden," she whispered to no one.

A hand softly touched her shoulder. Emilia looked up into Arthur's wrinkled face. A breeze coming in through a window stirred his white hair.

"Unlearning all you know is not for the faint of

heart," the old man said in a soft voice. "But unless you release everything you think you know and become like a little child, you can't enter the kingdom. It is as Justin taught."

His words made no sense to her. The Order preached the law, which required knowing that law inside and out, but Arthur's voice was reassuring. Emilia hadn't known either of her grandfathers well. One she'd had no relationship with and the other had passed when she was only four. Still, Arthur felt comforting and safe, as she imagined a good grandfather would.

He turned toward the elders, staying by her side.

"I think we have put this girl through enough. We should give her time to process," he said.

"We still haven't decided what to do with her," Bastien objected.

"I agree with Arthur," Torey said. "Emilia needs time and rest."

"She's only thirteen, Bastien," Helen said. "Be reasonable."

Bastien opened his mouth to rebuke them but then held his tongue. He closed his eyes and exhaled before resting his hands on the table and standing. "Very well. Then we will conclude this gathering."

Everyone started to stir, but Bastien wasn't done.

"Emilia Harker." His voice was stern. "What

Chapter 12

you've learned today would destroy every person in Zion if you shared it outside this mountain. Do you understand?"

Emilia nodded. She did understand.

"You'll forgive me in advance if I keep my eye on you," he said. "You may leave."

She stood shakily to her feet and moved toward the stairs. She wanted to run from the building, but she made herself walk until she was outside. Then she was running west to the fields, away from the elders. Away from what she had just learned. Away from her pain.

Away from it all.

CHAPTER 13

EMILIA RAN TILL HER LEGS BURNED and her lungs ached. She burst into the golden field and ignored the way the high grass slapped at her legs. Under the cover of the orchard shade, Emilia slowed, gasping for air. Tears moistened her cheeks and her sobs made breathing nearly impossible.

She bent over, her left hand on her knee, her right gripping a tree to support her. She tried to catch her breath but couldn't seem to. She sank to the ground at the tree's base and wept.

For the loss of her father. For the loss of her mother. For the loss of the world as she had always known it.

There is more to this world than you know. She'd wanted to understand why her father spoke those words to her, but now she just wanted to forget it all. She wanted to go back in time. Rewrite her story so it made sense. Erase the word *dragon* that bounced inside her skull like a rubber ball.

Emilia sniffed as her tears slowed and wind dried the streaks on her cheeks. She laid her head against the trunk, letting the morning air wash through her lungs. Cows mooed nearby, and she wondered how long she could be gone before a search party would come after her.

You'll forgive me if I keep an eye on you. Bastien's voice rumbled through her thoughts. He didn't trust her. Maybe he shouldn't. They'd entrusted their deepest secrets to her. They had a *dragon*! It was inside an egg, but still a dragon. A dragon they expected would hatch.

It was impossible not to wonder what the Grand Master would give her for that information.

She also knew where the Guardians were hiding—in a mountain, three days south of Capital City. Emilia could hand them over and maybe save her mother. She didn't care that she was in the bloodline of their true prophet. She owed them nothing.

If she chose her mother over the lives of the hundred and fifty people who lived in this mountain, what would her mother think of her? Hot emotion burned her face because Emilia knew how her mother would react.

She could hear her mother's voice whispering in

Chapter 13

the wind. *I raised you to be good and kind. What have you done?*

Emilia swallowed and snuffed the voice out. If Emilia did nothing, her mother might be killed. Wasn't it better to keep her alive, even if she was disappointed?

"Emilia?"

The voice caught her off guard and she jumped to her feet. Oliver stood a few yards off watching her. She hadn't even heard him approach. She wiped the back of her hand across her cheeks and cleared her throat. She must look a mess.

"I didn't mean to scare you," he said.

"Then what did you mean to do?" she returned. She knew her voice was unkind, but for one moment she didn't want to care.

He stayed where he was and shoved his hands into his pockets. "I came looking for you."

"Of course you did. They have to keep an eye on me, so I don't run into the desert and tell everyone you're hiding a dragon in your mountain."

His eyes flashed with surprise. "They told you?"

He knew. She rebuked her own foolishness. Of course, he knew. She didn't understand why she thought he should've told her. He owed her as little as she owed him. She was being unreasonable.

"A golden dragon egg, yes," Emilia said. Silence fell

between them. The sound of chickens happily clucking drifted past them, oblivious to heartache. Emilia had never wished she was a chicken until now.

"I should . . ." Emilia said with a heavy exhale.

"What?" Oliver said and took a step closer.

"I should tell the Order."

His chin flexed but he held his tongue.

"They have my mother, you know. Surely, I could trade your secrets for her. Isn't that what you would do to save your mother? Even if it meant . . ." Her words died.

Nothing but air filled the space between them.

"I would've done anything to save my mother," Oliver said. The pain in his voice touched her own. "I miss her every day." Oliver pressed the knuckle at the base of right his thumb to his lips, then his forehead and heart.

"What does that mean?" Emilia asked pointing towards his hand.

"It's a promise we made to those we've lost, to honor them with our words, thoughts, and hearts. We don't believe people leave us when they die. We lay their bodies to rest, but their love stays with us. It watches over us and lives through us until we see them again."

The notion was beautiful.

"What does the Order believe about those who leave

Chapter 13

us?" Oliver asked. The innocent question created a hollowness in her gut.

"Nothing, I guess." She didn't want to believe there was *nothing*. She looked up at Oliver. "Do you think my father is with me?"

He offered a half smile. "Yes, I do."

Emilia wanted it to be true, but she wasn't sure it was. She felt similarly about many of the Guardians' ways. They were beautiful and powerful but foreign, even opposed to what she'd been raised to believe. Accepting their beliefs would be like throwing out her childhood. Her foundation.

But they had a *dragon*. Their ancestors had fought alongside dragons. Were dragons allies, or evil creatures who hated humans? Someone was lying to her. How was she supposed to know the truth?

"Have you seen the dragon egg?" Emilia asked.

Oliver nodded.

"So, you know where it is?"

He paused at this. "You're going to ask me to take you to see it, aren't you?"

She didn't respond because a part of her was afraid to see anything even related to dragons of any kind. Another part of her had to see the egg, just to know if it really was true.

"You know I can't do that," he said, looking away.

"Why?"

He opened his mouth and then closed it.

"So, you don't trust me either?" Emilia asked.

He huffed. "You just told me you're going to tell the Order about the dragon."

"No, I said I *should*."

He ran his fingers through his hair and shook his head. "The elders would never allow it."

Emilia couldn't really blame them. She was a stranger, and they'd been protecting the egg for over a hundred years. *A dragon egg*. Five days ago, she would have called that forbidden fiction. Today, her pulse raced, and her heart thundered. Emilia needed to see it with her eyes to convince herself it was real.

She'd never been a rule breaker. But so much had changed. She had changed. She fiddled with the hem of her tunic and nibbled the inside of her bottom lip. "Maybe we could not tell them," Emilia whispered.

Oliver glanced up at her. "Go against the elders?"

"They didn't *specifically* say, 'Don't show Emilia the egg.'"

"It's implied," Oliver said.

He was right, but she needed him. The elders would never take her, and she knew she would never find it on her own. The cave system in this mountain was vast. The people of Zion would ensure the egg was hidden well. She wouldn't even know where to start.

Chapter 13

But the Order would surely return her mother in exchange for its location.

Emilia shut the idea out, refusing to think about it now. Honestly, she wasn't sure she could betray the Guardians. She would make that call later.

First, she had to see the dragon egg. She was sure about that now.

"Do you know that even saying the word *dragon* aloud can get you arrested in Capital City?" Emilia said.

Oliver watched her, his dark brown eyes thoughtful.

"Five days ago, I was certain about how the world worked," she continued. "I knew what was real. What was right. What was wrong. Now, I don't feel like I understand anything." Emilia took a step toward Oliver. "Please, I need to know I can believe you. How am I supposed to know what's true unless I see it myself?"

Oliver's eyes were shifting, taking in what she said. He was considering it, Emilia thought. He *wanted* to show her. Only his loyalty to Zion held him back. The breeze rustled his curly hair as he held her gaze.

He shifted on his feet and began to turn away from her. "Come on," he said. "We should get back."

He took a step and Emilia thought to say more but then reconsidered. A small voice warned her to leave it at that. She'd planted the seed. Now she needed to wait and see what grew from it.

The Golden Egg

✦✦✦

The sun was high, warming Emilia's skin as she rolled up her sleeves and continued washing freshly pulled carrots in the basket beside her. Izzy stood on the other side of Emilia, washing dirt off a bundle of cucumbers Maria had brought to the well a few minutes earlier.

The girls had been cleaning vegetables for over an hour, and Emilia's fingers were wrinkled. But the water was cool and gave her something to focus on as she tried to banish the idea of dragons.

She hadn't seen Oliver since he led her back to town, and she was starting to worry that maybe she'd gone too far.

"Okay, would you rather be stranded in the desert or lost on the ocean?" Izzy asked.

This game she called Would You Rather had begun about twenty minutes ago, after Izzy had exhausted all the questions she could think of about Capital City and Emilia's life.

"Both of those sound terrible," Emilia said.

Izzy stopped washing to give Emilia a sympathetic look. "Maybe you don't understand how this game works."

Emilia chuckled. Izzy had personality, that was for sure.

Chapter 13

"I guess I'd rather be stuck in the desert," Emilia said.

"Yeah, I agree. Mostly because I don't know how to swim, so being stuck on the ocean would end badly."

Emilia laughed again. Spoken like a girl far older than eight, she thought.

"Izzy," Amos called from a short distance off. "Rosey's wandered off again, insufferable chicken. She only comes back when you call."

"Oh, poor Rosey," Izzy exclaimed.

Emilia had learned that not only did Izzy speak with the flowers, but she was also a chicken whisperer. She had named them all after plants of some kind, and Emilia couldn't help but wonder how the girl reacted when Zion decided to eat one.

Izzy turned to Emilia. "This is an emergency. I have to go." The child plopped off the stepstool she was using to reach the well's water and ran off after her father. Emilia couldn't help but smile as she continued washing the last few carrots.

A shadow fell across the well. She looked up to see Oliver. He grabbed a cucumber and dipped it into the well's water before taking a bite. Emilia stared at him for a moment and then returned her eyes to the work at hand.

He glanced around, then spoke, keeping his voice to a near whisper. "Meet me at the southwestern end of the volcano, behind the last row of apple trees. Wait till the sun marks midday."

"Meet you? What for?"

He shrugged. "You know..."

Emilia's heart raced. The dragon egg?

"Oh. Oh, okay," she returned.

He nodded. "Good. If anyone asks, you're going to collect apples for the Sunday feast pies. We'll get some on the way, so it's not a lie."

She gave a brief nod as he took another bite of the cucumber, eyes twinkling. Without another word he grabbed a basket full of vegetables and walked toward the Community Hall, leaving Emilia at the well.

CHAPTER 14

EMILIA DID EXACTLY AS OLIVER ASKED. Basket in hand, she crossed the last line of apple trees and saw the rocky cliff that towered toward the clouds. She'd feared that if anyone stopped her while she was leaving camp, they would notice the sweat gathering at her temples or the shake in her hands. But no one had.

The sun hung in the middle of the sky. Emilia hoped she was on time. A branch snapped she swiveled toward the sound, fear building in her throat. Oliver stepped around a thick tree, a small pack strapped across his shoulders. He looked concerned and kept glancing over his shoulder as if to ensure he wasn't being followed.

"Are you going to make me regret this?" he asked.

Emilia didn't know what to say. The truth was, she

didn't know. She shook her head, because technically, it wasn't a lie.

Yet.

"Stay close and keep up," he said. With a final look over his shoulder, he started for the cliff, which was covered in thick ivy. Emilia looked back and saw the orchard blocked her view of the camp. She hoped that meant no one could see them either.

Oliver hurried to the cliff and pushed his hand through the thick ivy. He searched for a moment and then pulled on something Emilia couldn't see. The ivy split down the center creating a four-foot gap. Behind it, where she had expected to see a rock, was a cave entrance, dark as night.

Emilia watched, intrigued as Oliver moved into the opening. She followed with a final glance over her shoulder. Inside, Oliver knelt and yanked the pack from his back, then rummaged the pockets and pulled out a lighter. He moved to the cave wall, where a short barrel filled with torches sat. Beside it, a steel bucket was half filled with liquid. It smelled like fuel. Probably kerosene, the most common fuel for lamps.

Oliver dipped one end of the torch into the bucket, then set it ablaze. Light filled the small cave.

"Push that back into the wall," Oliver instructed, pointing to a small wooden lever. She did, and the

Chapter 14

wall of ivy fell back into place. She stood in awe for a beat. Turning to see flamelight warm Oliver's face, she couldn't help but smile.

"Cool, huh?" Oliver said.

"Yeah," she replied.

"The elders have created several escape routes with these secret mechanisms, just in case."

"In case of what?"

"Enemies ever find us," he said. "Enemies like the Order. So please tell me that you won't betray us. I'm doing this so you won't."

The air suddenly felt too thick to breathe.

"Show me the egg," she finally said.

He dipped his head. "That's what I'm doing. Just please—"

"Just show me and we'll go from there," she interrupted.

He stared at her for a moment. "Let's go." He headed deeper into the cave. She stayed close behind.

"How far are we going?" Emilia asked.

"It's about a three-hour trek."

Great.

"Don't worry, I brought snacks," he teased with a wink. It lightened the mood. A thought struck her. Oliver was becoming her friend. Guilt rolled through her gut. How could she betray a friend? Emilia shook off the thought and focused on her feet as they crossed the uneven ground.

Similar to the tunnel system behind the waterfall, this cave led to several tunnels. Oliver passed the first two and ducked into the farthest one.

"This way."

"Where do the others lead?" Emilia asked, catching up to him.

"Deeper into the mountain. The system is complex. It runs all the way through to the other side of Mount Zion, south. But I've never traveled that far. It's too dangerous."

"Why? What's south of Zion?"

"The Marauders."

A shiver tickled Emilia's spine. "Have you ever met a Marauder?"

"No, but before our ancestors found Mount Zion, both the Marauders and the Order hunted them. The Marauders come from a long line of dragon worshipers called the Scalers. They hated the Silver dragons and the Seers who stood with them."

Emilia stopped. "There's so much about this world I don't know."

He nodded as if he understood, though she doubted he did. "We have to move quick," he said. "We're going to be cutting it close to get back before dark."

Chapter 14

She nodded and then followed him down the tunnel.

✦✦✦

They'd exited the cave system an hour earlier, high above the valley, and taken a treacherous path up the mountain. A fall would prove deadly, but the path was wide and Emilia stayed away from the edge. They hiked up the jagged mountainside for another hour, sweat glistening across Emilia's forehead. She tried not to think about how they would have to travel back down this same path. She wasn't used to this kind of danger.

"We're close," Oliver said as they approached a large boulder. "Help me with this."

It took their combined strength to move the rock and uncover another wooden lever. Oliver yanked it down, and a slight rumble shook their heels. A wide bush on the opposite side of the boulder slid out of the way, revealing a two-foot-wide, four-foot-tall gap in the mountainside.

Oliver stooped and entered the crack, Emilia following closely. The long passage darkened as they traveled and she wondered if they might get stuck, but eventually they spilled out into a wide space open to the sky. Relief filled her.

The Golden Egg

They stood on a ten-foot-wide ledge. An old, wooden, plank bridge crossed a chasm to another ledge. Only two thick ropes served as handrails. A gust of wind caused the whole bridge to sway, and Emilia's stomach dropped.

"Come on." Oliver eased himself onto the bridge. Heights didn't bother Emilia, but the swaying bridge looked too weak to hold their weight. When Oliver put his full weight on the first board, it creaked like it might snap.

He glanced back, a bit of the color leaving his face, and feigned a smile. "It's safe."

She wasn't sure if he said that for her sake or his. But this bridge was the only way across. Emilia kept her eyes up as she moved onto the planks, gripping the ropes on either side. The wind pulled at her hair, and she hesitated. Her fingers on the rope turned white. Instinctively, she glanced down.

They hovered over darkness, an endless pit. Emilia jerked her eyes back up to Oliver, who crossed the final plank and landed safely on the other side. She placed one foot ahead of the next. And then another. By the time her feet reached the far ledge, she thought she might vomit.

Oliver took her hand and pulled her away from the edge as Emilia took several shaky breaths and tried to

Chapter 14

steady her trembling bones.

"Sorry," he said. "I should've warned you about that."

"Anything else I should know about?" she tried to tease, but her voice came out like a scared squeak.

His cheeks reddened and he shrugged. "No one's ever fallen. It's just through here anyways."

Emilia looked past Oliver to see another small cave opening. It looked like an arched door cut into the stone, too smooth to be made by the earth's shifting. Oliver didn't have to tell her that's where they were headed.

Her body had calmed, and she followed Oliver into the cave. Slits in the rock overhead created pockets of natural light as they walked deeper into the tunnel. It wasn't too wide, maybe six feet across, and Emilia knew she could touch the stone overhead if she stood on her tiptoes. She looked up through an orange-sized hole that revealed the blue sky.

Emilia thought she saw something moving along the edge of the stone tunnel.

"I always forget how much colder it is in here," Oliver said as Emilia searched the dark crevice where she'd thought she saw the movement.

A rattle sounded and something suddenly struck out toward her. Emilia shrieked and jumped back, narrowly avoiding the creature's fangs. The viper was four or five feet long, thick with light brown scales and black stripes lining its body.

Oliver tried to slam his heel down on the creature, but it was too quick. It sent out a terrifying hiss that echoed around them, then coiled to strike in Oliver's direction.

"Oliver!" Emilia cried as the boy yanked a blade from the strap at his thigh. The snake shot forward and struck Oliver's leg. He cried in pain as the snake sank its bite into Oliver's ankle.

Oliver drove his blade through the snake's back and into the ground. The snake released Oliver and flailed, but the knife pinned it in place. A moment later its rattle stilled. Blood darkened the dirt under the snake's wound.

Emilia's wide eyes stared at the dead reptile. It had all happened so fast. Oliver moaned, snapping Emilia out of her shock. She rushed to Oliver, who had slumped against the stone wall, and dropped to her knees beside him.

"Oliver!"

"Help me up," he said.

She wrapped his arm around her shoulders and hoisted him onto his good leg. "We have to go back!"

He shook his head. "No, we're almost there. I'll be okay."

Chapter 14

"You sure?"

"Come on." He winced as he hobbled.

Within twenty feet they exited the tunnel and found themselves in a large cave.

"I need to get my boot and sock off to clean the wound," he said, leaning against the wall and sliding down to his seat. Emilia fumbled with his laces and tore the strings loose. She yanked the boot off.

He groaned.

"I'm sorry," she said.

"Here." He shrugged out of his pack. "Everything you need to clean the wound is inside."

"That was a rattlesnake, Oliver," Emilia said.

"I know," he said.

"Please tell me you have antivenom in here."

"Never leave home without it."

Emilia exhaled a breath of relief and emptied the contents of Oliver's pack onto the ground.

"Inside the white pouch," Oliver said. Sweat glistened on his forehead.

Although she'd never actually seen a rattlesnake until now, Emilia knew how quickly its venom worked. Within thirty minutes Oliver's ankle would be too swollen to move. Her father had been bitten when she was seven and he'd been in bed for two days before finding relief.

Emilia spotted the white pouch and yanked it open, quickly locating sterilized wipes, bandages and the antivenom.

Working as quickly as possible, Emilia cut a hole in Oliver's pants along his thigh, only an inch long, filled the syringe with the medication, and held her breath as she stabbed the needle into his skin. He bit back a cry and pressed the back of his head against the rock as she emptied the syringe into Oliver's leg.

She then set out to clean the wound, which had already started swelling, and dress it with clean bandages. Oliver's skin felt too warm already. There was no way they were headed back to Zion tonight. He wouldn't be able to stand, much less walk.

His breathing was even as he looked at his fat ankle and then up to Emilia's face. She held out a water canteen and he took it. "Thanks."

"I should be thanking you," she said sitting back on her heels. "The snake was coming for me, and you distracted it. If you hadn't done that, I'd probably be dead."

"Well, I doubt that, but that's what friends are for," he said with a grin.

She smiled as warmth spread through her chest. "Who would've thought that a Guardian and a follower of the Order could become friends."

He smiled back and then chuckled. "By the way,

Chapter 14

we're here."

She gave him a confused look, and he shoved his chin toward something behind her. Emilia looked over her shoulder and froze. She pushed off the ground and spun toward the center of the cave.

A single shaft of sunlight from a crack in the ceiling filled the large space with ethereal light. The cavern was empty except for a square altar about two feet tall in the cave's center. Nestled in a bed of dried grass lay something Emilia would have sworn couldn't exist.

She took cautious steps forward, unblinking as her eyes drank in the wonder. It wasn't decorated or surrounded by lush fabrics. Nobody knelt before it or danced around. It was humble. Simple. But in that moment Emilia knew it changed everything.

She was looking at a large, golden, oval sphere.

An egg.

And just beyond it, painstakingly engraved into the cave wall by an artisan's skilled hands, a large, circular icon about 3 feet in diameter. The etching in the circle was a plain silhouette but polished so that it almost glowed in the dim light, revealing the image in unmistakable clarity.

It was a dragon.

Emilia lowered her eyes back to the golden egg.

It could be nothing other than a dragon's egg.

CHAPTER 15

EMILIA COULDN'T TAKE HER EYES off the golden dragon egg, even after thirty minutes, during which Oliver explained how his people had guarded this single egg for generations. Touching it was forbidden, he said, and she'd gladly kept her distance. It felt so wrong. But it also felt so right.

Wrong in that its very existence overturned so much of what she'd held sacred. Right in that it meant her father was right—the dragon egg was right here.

"Is there anything living inside?" she asked.

"They say so," he replied.

"But how does it stay alive?"

"No one knows, but they say unhatched dragons have power to live for a thousand years."

"It all seems so impossible," she whispered.

"That it's still alive?" he asked.

"That it even exists, but yes, that too. It feels like we shouldn't be here."

"Well, we shouldn't. But I'm doing this so you won't betray us, remember?"

Yes, there was that. She had no idea what she would do now.

"We'll spend the night here and return in the morning," he said. "We need to make a fire."

Emilia followed his laborious instructions on how to build a fire. She glared at him more than once as she tried and failed several times to ignite the kindling. Finally, a flame caught, and she piled wood stored in the cavern on top until they had a fire large enough to warm their corner of the cave.

They ate the snacks he'd brought, then Oliver settled into a feverish sleep. Emilia eased his blanket up to his chin and tucked it behind his shoulders, then returned to her side of the fire.

She stoked the flames, hoping to maintain the fire as long as she could. The sky through the cave's ceiling was dark and Emilia tried to banish the fears of what creatures might find their way into the cave during the night hours. Her thoughts turned to Marauders and snakes.

Maybe the Guardians would come looking for them when Torey realized they were missing. Had Oliver

Chapter 15

told anyone where they were going? Maybe Brodie. It seemed like something Oliver might do. He was smart, his pack filled with essentials. If nobody came, they would hobble their way back to Zion in the morning, but that would take forever with Oliver's swollen leg.

Eventually, her eyes started to feel heavy. She fought to keep them open but lost the battle and fell asleep beside the dying fire.

In her dream, Emilia found herself back in the Capital City courtroom, both her parents blindfolded on the platform. The Grand Master entered with the silver knife in hand. His empty words pounded inside Emilia's mind. Black snakes followed him, and Emilia watched as they slithered toward her parents' feet. They coiled around her mother's ankles and wound up her father's legs. One of them sank their venomous fangs into her father's leg and he cried out.

Emilia tried to tear herself from the bench but knew it was futile. If she'd kept her mouth shut and not told Ruth about the dragon talk, none of this would have happened. She'd still be with her parents in their humble two-bedroom home, laughing while they made dinner. Instead, she faced the death of her father, her mother likely in chains, and this madness about dragons.

Emilia's eyes snapped open, and she sat up with

a start, heart racing. The cave was dark, and Oliver still slept. The pit between them held red coals, but the flames were gone. She wiped the back of her hand across her forehead and grabbed a stick near the fire pit.

She poked at the coals, hoping to rouse them back to life, when the strangest sensation brushed the back of her shoulders. She stilled and listened. Nothing. She turned slowly and looked around the cave. Without the sun shining through any cracks, she couldn't see anything that might be hiding in the shadows.

But she couldn't shake the feeling that something was here besides her and Oliver.

Emilia stood, her pulse pounding, and clenched the stick she'd been using. In the dead of night, the silence felt suffocating. Her eyes rested on the altar in the middle of the cave, where she could see the faintest outline of the dragon egg. Had somebody come to steal it? It was a strange thought. Stranger still was that it made her want to defend the egg.

Emilia released a long breath and tried to relax. Her mind was playing tricks on her. But she couldn't pull her eyes from the egg. She moved toward it like a moth to a flame, stopping when she was only a few feet away. Emilia cocked her head and stared at the egg.

Something about it seemed different. Or maybe it just *felt* different. Which was another weird thing to think. The egg was oval, maybe eighteen inches

Chapter 15

from end to end. The gold didn't shine like a coin might because the surface was rough, but it was most definitely gold.

She saw her hand extended toward the egg before she realized it had moved from her side. She yanked it back, scolding herself for being so juvenile.

But she couldn't deny that she wanted to touch it. Wanted to feel the shell beneath her fingertips. Was it just curiosity? What was it they said about curiosity killing the cat? She shook her head and took a small step back, thinking she needed to return to the protection of their fire.

The egg suddenly trembled for a moment and then stilled.

Emilia stopped breathing. Had that just happened? She waited for more movement, but nothing else happened. Slowly she released her breath and rebuked herself. She was only imagining things.

Just as she was about to turn, the egg began to tremble again, and this time she moved toward it without thinking, as if pulled by an unseen force.

A voice of reason shouted for her to stop. No matter what she did, she should not touch that egg. But another voice whispered like a soft and warm lullaby, wooing her, telling her she needed to touch the egg. Her life depended on it.

Before Emilia could stop herself, she reached out

The Golden Egg

and lay her hand against the shell. The moment her palm met the cool surface, it warmed. Then grew undeniably hot. Emilia gasped, yanked her hand back, and stumbled away. The surface her palm had touched started to glow.

A crack cut the silence, and she watched in shock as a fissure split the face of the egg. It spread in both directions, and wisps of light leaked out like golden smoke until the crack reached the top of the egg, where it stopped.

Bright rays poured from the fissure and surrounded the shell until the whole egg disappeared behind a spinning white cloud. Light suddenly erupted from the egg and filled the room. Emilia instinctively ducked. The fire in the pit behind her sprang to life once again.

And then the white light was gone, leaving the cave to glow by the flames of the fire now blazing behind her.

She stood and stared at the egg. But there *was* no egg!

In its place, a small creature uncurled and stretched its back like a cat. It pushed its front legs against the straw nest and sat, raising its head to look at Emilia.

Emilia gawked in disbelief. It was a baby dragon.

For a few long seconds that might have stretched into a full minute, Emilia and the dragon just stared at one another without moving.

Emilia could barely make out the tiny dragon's

Chapter 15

features in the dim firelight. The first thing she noticed was the dragon wasn't gold. Its scales were a light gray. Its eyes were dark and unblinking as it wagged its head back and forth, studying her. The dragon sat about two feet tall with a thin tail that curled around its feet. Small nubs protruded from either side of its back.

That's where its wings will grow, she thought. Because this was a dragon.

Emilia stepped back; her mind unable to process what was happening.

"Emilia," a voice called. Oliver's voice.

She turned and saw him staring wide-eyed from where he sat across the cavern. She could see how pale his face had become.

The dragon gave a slight screech, and she turned to see the dragon standing now, its eyes trained on Emilia. It squeaked at her again and tilted its head as if trying to tell her something.

Before Emilia could respond, another voice emerged from the tunnel. "Oliver! Emilia!"

It was some distance off. Emilia looked back at Oliver, still staring at the hatched dragon, who had gone still like a statue.

More voices joined the first and echoes of footsteps filled the cave as a figure burst from the tunnel, a torch in hand. Torey.

Relief flooded Emilia before she remembered that

The Golden Egg

a baby dragon stood behind her. Torey saw Emilia and then scanned the cave without even noticing the dragon. She must have been blocking it from his view.

His eyes found his son and he rushed over. "Oliver."

Torey broke Oliver's trance. The boy turned to greet his panicked father. "I'm okay, Dad. Just a rattlesnake bite."

Torey responded in shock, but Emilia had stopped listening because the dragon had hopped out of its nest and was at her feet, rubbing against her leg. Emilia shrieked and jumped back, her heart crashing inside her chest.

The small dragon sat back, looked up at Emilia, and screeched. Emilia didn't know what it wanted from her. She didn't speak dragon.

"What is this?" a harsh voice spat.

Four more Guardians had joined them. The riders Marcs and Saul, and the elders Amos and Bastien. All of them held torches, flooding the cavern with light and shadows.

As one, they stared at the baby dragon at Emilia's feet. A mix of emotions played across their faces. Anger, surprise, delight, terror, confusion.

The dragon must have sensed something was wrong because it moved closer to Emilia and growled at the others, a slight but deadly threat that vibrated from its throat.

Chapter 15

Bastien, protector of the Guardians, took a step forward, his eyes on the creature. The baby dragon snapped its jaws at him, and he stilled. He looked at Emilia as if she were the enemy.

"What in God's holy name have you done?" he whispered.

Emilia fought to breathe through her panic.

"What happened?" Bastien demanded, more forceful now.

Again, the dragon hissed and growled as if defending her.

"I . . . I touched the egg," Emilia said.

Soft voices of confusion filled the cave.

"No," Bastien said, voice raised above the others. "This must be a mistake. You're lying."

"She's not," Oliver said. His father had helped him to his feet. Thankfully, the antivenom was working and his swelling had apparently eased. "Why would she lie about this?"

"The prophecy is clear, Bastien," Torey said, stepping past the protector. "The egg will choose its rider and hatch only for that one soul."

Emilia blinked, unable to process what that meant.

"You can't possibly think that this girl from Capital City is the dragon rider!" Bastien snapped. "The chosen one must be a Guardian within the . . ." His words died off.

"Within the bloodline of a true Seer," Torey finished.

It took Emilia another moment to realize they were talking about her sharing the bloodline of the true prophet.

The dragon forced itself between her feet and curled its tail around her right ankle. It watched everyone carefully, ready to protect her if needed.

Reality slowly settled on her shoulders, and the implications of what Torey had said flooded her all at once.

She had touched the egg, and after a hundred years of waiting it had hatched. *For her.* The dragon had chosen her to be its rider.

"I can't be a dragon rider," she said. "I . . . No . . . This is a mistake."

Torey and Oliver moved closer to her, and Emilia searched their faces for a way out.

"The dragon has been waiting for you, Emilia Harker. It chose you," Torey said.

Frightened tears sprang to her eyes. "What if I don't want to be chosen?"

Torey's eyes softened and he smiled. His eyes were also flush with tears, but they were tears of joy. "The chosen often don't."

Movement at her feet drew her gaze down. The small dragon had lain its forehead against the inside of

Chapter 15

her leg and warmth began to spread up her body. The warmth was mixed with a calming sensation that filled her mind with wonder.

The cave faded and the dragon lifted its eyes to meet hers. For a moment, those eyes shone with a love and knowing that seemed to reach into her very bones. It was all absurd, she thought, but even thinking that, she realized her heart wanted to believe in this dragon.

"Enough," Bastien said.

His words broke the wonder the dragon had cast over Emilia.

"We'll take the girl and dragon before the elders," Bastien said. "They will settle this."

Emilia felt Bastien's gaze and dared to look at him. His expression was clear. The dragon may have hatched at her touch, but he would never accept her as its rider.

She wanted to tell him not to worry. Regardless of their prophecy about the golden dragon and its rider, regardless of the warmth of having the dragon close, regardless of the hope she saw in others' eyes . . .

Regardless, she would never be their dragon rider.

CHAPTER 16

F AR AWAY IN THE KEEP of the dragon queen, Victoria woke in the dead of night, acutely aware that the dragon mother was summoning her. Without a moment's delay, she scurried from the bed and threw on a heavy housecoat before grabbing a lantern and heading to wake Lee. She had planned to return to Capital City in the morning, but she was at her queen's disposal, and her queen beckoned her to come.

Now.

She left her room and flew downstairs to the lower floor. Lee's room was first on the right, and she tapped her knuckles against his door. A moment passed, then she heard the shuffling of feet. The door opened and Lee's sleepy face appeared in the flamelight.

"I'm being summoned," Victoria said and then turned, knowing Lee would follow without question. They descended another set of stairs into the sanctuary.

The Golden Egg

A few minutes later Victoria strode across the dragon's lair and felt the rumble of its heavy approach. She saw the faint purple glow before the dragon came into view, and as soon as it did, she bowed in honor.

The egg has woken, the dragon queen said in her mind. *The golden dragon has hatched.*

Victoria felt ice fill her veins. "How?"

Its rider has been chosen. Time is of the essence.

Victoria swallowed her fear and steeled her face. "Are you sure, my queen?"

Are you questioning my ability to sense my enemy?

"No, my queen. Forgive me."

Your forgiveness will be earned when you destroy the dragon and its rider. It cannot be allowed to grow into its fullness. I can sense it clearly, which means that it must be close.

Victoria's mind spun. For a moment, she didn't know what to think. But her confusion was replaced by the conviction that her time had finally come. The dragon was here, and she would be the Overseer to save them all from it.

"More confirmation that the Guardians are closer than we thought," she said, speaking the obvious and immediately regretting it.

The queen ignored her comment.

Find them, the dragon and its rider. Kill them both if you hope to live.

To Be Continued in

BOOK TWO

The Unknown Path

MORE ADVENTURES AWAIT

THE IMPOSSIBLE PLACES SERIES

Journey to Impossible Places

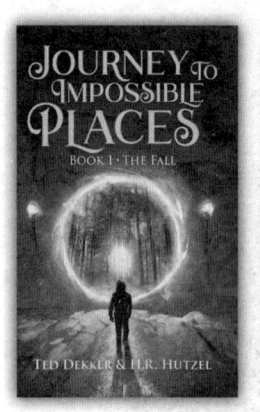

World of Impossible Things

WWW.TEDDEKKER.COM

Discover the entire
Dekker young reader universe.

THE DRAGONS SERIES

And They Found Dragons

The Dragons Among Us

WWW.TEDDEKKER.COM

THE DREAM TRAVELERS SERIES

The Dream Travelers Quest

The Dream Travelers Game

WWW.TEDDEKKER.COM

THE MILLIE MAVEN SERIES

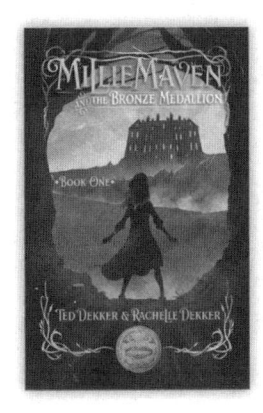

THE DRAGON RIDER SERIES

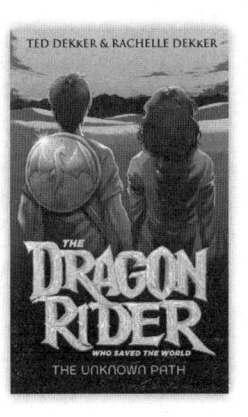

WHICH ADVENTURE WILL YOU CHOOSE?

WWW.TEDDEKKER.COM